AFTER A SHADOW

AND OTHER STORIES

T. S. ARTHUR

After A Shadow

Thomas Anderton

PO Box 2211
Fairfield, IA 52556
www.1stworldlibrary.org
First Edition

LCCN: 2004195359

Softcover ISBN: 1-4218-0193-0
Hardcover ISBN: 1-4218-0093-4
eBook ISBN: 1-4218-0293-7

Purchase *"After A Shadow"*
as a traditional bound book at:
www.1stWorldLibrary.org/purchase.asp?ISBN=1-4218-0193-0

1st World Library Literary Society is a nonprofit organization dedicated to promoting literacy by:

- Creating a free internet library accessible from any computer worldwide.
- Hosting writing competitions and offering book publishing scholarships.

Readers interested in supporting literacy through sponsorship, donations or membership please contact: literacy@1stworldlibrary.org
Check us out at: www.1stworldlibrary.ORG and start downloading free ebooks today.

After A Shadow

contributed by Tim, Ed & Rodney

in support of

1st World Library Literary Society

CONTENTS

I

AFTER A SHADOW

"ARTY! Arty!" called Mrs. Mayflower, from the window, one bright June morning. "Arty, darling! What is the child after? Just look at him, Mr. Mayflower!"

I leaned from the window, in pleasant excitement, to see what new and wonderful performance had been attempted by my little prodigy - my first born - my year old bud of beauty, the folded leaves in whose bosom were just beginning to loosen themselves, and send out upon the air sweet intimations of an abounding fragrance. He had escaped from his nurse, and was running off in the clear sunshine, the slant rays of which threw a long shadow before him.

"Arty, darling!" His mother's voice flew along and past his ear, kissing it in gentle remonstrance as it went by. But baby was in eager pursuit of something, and the call, if heard, was unheeded. His eyes were opening world-ward, and every new phenomenon - commonplace and unheeded by us - that addressed itself to his senses, became a wonder and a delight. Some new object was drawing him away from the loving heart and protecting arm.

"Run after him, Mr. Mayflower!" said my wife, with a touch of anxiety in her voice. "He might fall and hurt himself."

I did not require a second intimation as to my duty in the case. Only a moment or two elapsed before I was on the pavement, and making rapid approaches towards my truant boy.

"What is it, darling? What is Arty running after?" I said, as I laid my hand on his arm, and checked his eager speed. He struggled a moment, and then stood still, stooping forward for something on the ground.

"O, papa see!" There was a disappointed and puzzled look in his face as he lifted his eyes to mine. He failed to secure the object of his pursuit.

"What is it, sweet?" My eyes followed his as they turned upon the ground.

He stooped again, and caught at something; and again looked up in a perplexed, half-wondering way.

"Why, Arty!" I exclaimed, catching him up in my arms. "It's only your shadow! Foolish child!" And I ran back to Mrs. Mayflower, with my baby-boy held close against my heart.

"After a shadow!" said I, shaking my head, a little soberly, as I resigned Arty to his mother. "So life begins - and so it ends! Poor Arty!"

Mrs. Mayflower laughed out right merrily.

"After a shadow! Why, darling!" And she kissed and

hugged him in overflowing tenderness.

"So life begins - so it ends," I repeated to myself, as I left the house, and walked towards my store. "Always in pursuit of shadows! We lose to-day's substantial good for shadowy phantoms that keep our eyes ever in advance, and our feet ever hurrying forward. No pause - no ease - no full enjoyment of *now*. O, deluded heart! - ever bartering away substance for shadow!"

I grow philosophic sometimes. Thought will, now and then, take up a passing incident, and extract the moral. But how little the wiser are we for moralizing! we look into the mirror of truth, and see ourselves - then turn away, and forget what manner of men we are. Better for us if it were not so; if we remembered the image that held our vision.

The shadow lesson was forgotten by the time I reached my store, and thought entered into business with its usual ardor. I buried myself, amid letters, invoices, accounts, samples, schemes for gain, and calculations of profit. The regular, orderly progression of a fair and well-established business was too slow for my out-reaching desires. I must drive onward at a higher speed, and reach the goal of wealth by a quicker way. So my daily routine was disturbed by impatient aspirations. Instead of entering, in a calm self-possession of every faculty, into the day's appropriate work, and finding, in its right performance, the tranquil state that ever comes as the reward of right-doing in the right place, I spent the larger part of this day in the perpetration of a plan for increasing my gains beyond, anything heretofore achieved.

"Mr. Mayflower," said one of the clerks, coming back

to where I sat at my private desk, busy over my plan, "we have a new man in from the West; a Mr. B - , from Alton. He wants to make a bill of a thousand dollars. Do you know anything about him?"

Now, even this interruption annoyed me. What was a new customer and a bill of a thousand dollars to me just at that moment of time? I saw tens of thousands in prospective.

"Mr. B -, of Alton?" said I, affecting an effort of memory. "Does he look like a fair man?"

"I don't recall him. Mr. B -? Hum-m-m. He impresses you favorably, Edward?"

"Yes, sir; but it may be prudent to send and get a report."

"I'll see to that, Edward," said I. "Sell him what he wants. If everything is not on the square, I'll give you the word in time. It's all right, I've no doubt."

"He's made a bill at Kline & Co.'s, and wants his goods sent there to be packed," said my clerk.

"Ah, indeed! Let him have what he wants, Edward. If Kline & Co. sell him, we needn't hesitate."

And turning to my desk, my plans, and my calculations, I forgot all about Mr. B -, and the trifling bill of a thousand dollars that he proposed buying. How clear the way looked ahead! As thought created the means of successful adventure, and I saw myself moving forward and grasping results, the whole circle of life took a quicker motion, and my mind rose into a pleasant enthusiasm. Then I grew impatient for the initiatory steps that were to come, and felt as if the to-morrow, in which they must be taken, would never appear. A day seemed like a week or a month.

Six o'clock found me in not a very satisfactory state of mind. The ardor of my calculations had commenced abating. Certain elements, not seen and considered in the outset, were beginning to assume shape and consequence, and to modify, in many essential particulars, the grand result towards which I had been looking with so much pleasure. Shadowy and indistinct became the landscape, which seemed a little while before so fair and inviting. A cloud settled down upon it here, and a cloud there, breaking up its unity, and destroying much of its fair proportion. I was no longer mounting up, and moving forwards on the light wing of a castle-building imagination, but down upon the hard, rough ground, coming back into the consciousness that all progression, to be sure, must be slow and toilsome.

I had the afternoon paper in my hands, and was running my eyes up and down the columns, not reading, but, in a half-absent way, trying to find something of sufficient interest to claim attention, when, among the money and business items, I came upon a paragraph that sent the declining thermometer of my feelings away down towards the chill of zero. It touched, in the most vital part, my scheme of gain; and the shrinking bubble burst.

"Have the goods sold to that new customer from Alton been delivered?" I asked, as the real interest of my wasted day loomed up into sudden importance.

"Yes, sir," was answered by one of my clerks; "they were sent to Kline & Co.'s immediately. Mr. B - said they were packing up his goods, which were to be shipped to-day."

"He's a safe man, I should think. Kline & Co. sell him." My voice betrayed the doubt that came stealing over me like a chilly air.

"They sell him only for cash," said my clerk. "I saw one of their young men this afternoon, and asked after Mr. B -'s standing. He didn't know anything about him; said B - was a new man, who bought a moderate cash bill, but was sending in large quantities of goods to be packed - five or six times beyond the amount of his purchases with them."

"Is that so!" I exclaimed, rising to my feet, all awake now to the real things which I had permitted a shadow to obscure.

"Just what he told me," answered my clerk.

"It has a bad look," said I. "How large a bill did he make with us?"

The sales book was referred to. "Seventeen hundred dollars," replied the clerk.

"What! I thought he was to buy only to the amount of a thousand dollars?" I returned, in surprise and dismay.

"You seemed so easy about him, sir," replied the clerk, "that I encouraged him to buy; and the bill ran up more heavily than I was aware until the footing gave exact figures."

I drew out my watch. It was close on to half past six.

"I think, Edward," said I, "that you'd better step round to Kline & Co.'s, and ask if they've shipped B -'s goods yet. If not, we'll request them to delay long enough in the morning to give us time to sift the matter. If B -'s after a swindling game, we'll take a short course, and save our goods."

"It's too late," answered my clerk. "B - called a little after one o'clock, and gave notes for the amount of his bill. He was to leave in the five o'clock line for Boston."

I turned my face a little aside, so that Edward might not see all the anxiety that was pictured there.

"You look very sober, Mr. Mayflower," said my good wife, gazing at me with eyes a little shaded by concern, as I sat with Arty's head leaning against my bosom that evening; "as sober as baby looked this morning, after his fruitless shadow chase."

"And for the same reason," said I, endeavoring to speak calmly and firmly.

"Why, Mr. Mayflower!" Her face betrayed a rising anxiety. My assumed calmness and firmness did not wholly disguise the troubled feelings that lay, oppressively, about my heart.

"For the same reason," I repeated, steadying my voice, and trying to speak bravely. "I have been chasing a shadow all day; a mere phantom scheme of profit; and at night-fall I not only lose my shadow, but find my feet far off from the right path, and bemired. I called

Arty a foolish child this morning. I laughed at his mistake. But, instead of accepting the lesson it should have conveyed, I went forth and wearied myself with shadow-hunting all day."

Mrs. Mayflower sighed gently. Her soft eyes drooped away from my face, and rested for some moments on the floor.

"I am afraid we are all, more or less, in pursuit of shadows," she said, - "of the unreal things, projected by thought on the canvas of a too creative imagination. It is so with me; and I sigh, daily, over some disappointment. Alas! if this were all. Too often both the shadow-good and the real-good of to-day are lost. When night falls our phantom good is dispersed, and we sigh for the real good we might have enjoyed."

"Shall we never grow wiser?" I asked.

"We shall never grow happier unless we do," answered Mrs. Mayflower.

"Happiness!" I returned, as thought began to rise into clearer perception; "is it not the shadow after which we are all chasing, with such a blind and headlong speed?"

"Happiness is no shadow. It is a real thing," said Mrs. Mayflower. "It does not project itself in advance of us; but exists in the actual and the now, if it exists at all. We cannot catch it by pursuit; that is only a cheating counterfeit, in guilt and tinsel, which dazzles our eyes in the ever receding future. No; happiness is a state of life; and it comes only to those who do each day's work peaceful self-forgetfulness, and a calm trust in the Giver of all good for the blessing that lies stored for each one prepared to receive it in every hour of the coming time."

"Who so does each day's work in a peaceful self-forgetfulness and patient trust in God?" I said, turning my eyes away from the now tranquil face of Mrs. Mayflower.

"Few, if any, I fear," she answered; "and few, if any, are happy. The common duties and common things of our to-days look so plain and homely in their ungilded actualities, that we turn our thought and interest away from them, and create ideal forms of use and beauty, into which we can never enter with conscious life. We are always losing the happiness of our to-days; and our to-morrows never come."

I sighed my response, and sat for a long time silent. When the tea bell interrupted me from my reverie, Arty lay fast asleep on my bosom. As I kissed him on his way to his mother's arms, I said, -

"Dear baby! may it be your first and last pursuit of a shadow."

"No - no! Not yet, my sweet one!" answered Mrs. Mayflower, hugging him to her heart. "Not yet. We cannot spare you from our world of shadows."

II

IN THE WAY OF TEMPTATION

MARTIN GREEN was a young man of good habits and a good conceit of himself. He had listened, often and again, with as much patience as he could assume, to warning and suggestion touching the dangers that beset the feet of those who go out into this wicked world, and become subject to its legion of temptations. All these warnings and suggestions he considered as so many words wasted when offered to himself.

"I'm in no danger," he would sometimes answer to relative or friend, who ventured a remonstrance against certain associations, or cautioned him about visiting certain places.

"If I wish to play a game of billiards, I will go to a billiard saloon," was the firm position he assumed. "Is there any harm in billiards? I can't help it if bad men play at billiards, and congregate in billiard saloons. Bad men may be found anywhere and everywhere; on the street, in stores, at all public places, even in church. Shall I stay away from church because bad men are there?"

This last argument Martin Green considered unanswerable. Then he would say, -

"If I want a plate of oysters, I'll go to a refectory, and I'll take a glass of ale with my oysters, if it so pleases me. What harm, I would like to know? Danger of getting into bad company, you say? Hum-m! Complimentary to your humble servant! But I'm not the kind to which dirt sticks."

So, confident of his own power to stand safely in the midst of temptation, and ignorant of its thousand insidious approaches, Martin Green, at the age of twenty-one, came and went as he pleased, mingling with the evil and the good, and seeing life under circumstances of great danger to the pure and innocent. But he felt strong and safe, confident of neither stumbling nor falling. All around him he saw young men yielding to the pressure of temptation and stepping aside into evil ways; but they were weak and vicious, while he stood firm-footed on the rock of virtue!

It happened, very naturally, as Green was a bright, social young man, that he made acquaintances with other young men, who were frequently met in billiard saloons, theatre lobbies, and eating houses. Some of these he did not understand quite as well as he imagined. The vicious, who have ends to gain, know how to cloak themselves, and easily deceive persons of Green's character. Among, these acquaintances was a handsome, gentlemanly, affable young man, named Bland, who gradually intruded himself into his confidence. Bland never drank to excess, and never seemed inclined to sensual indulgences. He had, moreover, a way of moralizing that completely veiled his true quality from the not very penetrating Martin Green, whose shrewdness and knowledge of character were far less acute than he, in his self-conceit, imagined.

One evening, instead of going with his sister to the house of a friend, where a select company of highly-intelligent ladies and gentleman were to meet, and pass an evening together, Martin excused himself under the pretence of an engagement, and lounged away to an eating and drinking saloon, there to spend an hour in smoking, reading the newspapers, and enjoying a glass of ale, the desire for which was fast growing into a habit. Strong and safe as he imagined himself, the very fact of preferring the atmosphere of a drinking or billiard saloon to that in which refined and intellectual people breathe, showed that he was weak and in danger.

He was sitting with a cigar in his mouth, and a glass of ale beside him, reading with the air of a man who felt entirely satisfied with himself, and rather proud than ashamed of his position and surroundings, when his pleasant friend, Mr. Bland, crossed the room, and, reaching out his hand, said, with his smiling, hearty manner, -

"How are you, my friend? What's the news to-day?" And he drew a chair to the table, calling at the same time to a waiter for a glass of ale.

"I never drink anything stronger than ale," he added, in a confidential way, not waiting for Green to answer his first remark. "Liquors are so drugged nowadays, that you never know what poison you are taking; besides, tippling is a bad habit, and sets a questionable example. We must, you know, have some regard to the effect of our conduct on weaker people. Man is an imitative animal. By the way, did you see Booth's Cardinal Wolsey?"

"Yes."

"A splendid piece of acting, - was it not? You remember, after the cardinal's fall, that noble passage to which he gives utterance. It has been running through my mind ever since: - "'Mark but my fall, and that that ruined me.

Cromwell, I charge thee, fling away ambition:

By that sin fell the angels; how can man, then,

The image of his Maker, hope to win by't?

Love thyself last: Cherish those hearts that hate thee:

Corruption wins not more than honesty.

Still in thy right hand carry gentle peace,

To silence envious tongues; be just, and fear not.

Let all the ends thou aim'st at be thy country's,

Thy God's, and truth's; then if thou fall'st, O Cromwell,

Thou fall'st a blessed martyr.'

"'Love thyself last. - Let all the ends thou aim'st at be thy country's, thy God's, and truth's.' Could a man's whole duty in life be expressed in fewer words, or said more grandly? I think not."

And so he went on, charming the ears of Green, and inspiring him with the belief that he was a person of the purest instincts and noblest ends. While they talked, two young men, strangers to Green came up, and were introduced by Bland as "My very particular friends." Something about them did not at first impress Martin favorably. But this impression soon wore off, they were so intelligent and agreeable, Bland, after a little while, referred again to the Cardinal Wolsey of Booth, and, drawing a copy of Shakspeare's Henry VIII. from his pocket, remarked, -

"If it wasn't so public here, I'd like to read a few of the best passages in Wolsey's part."

"Can't we get a private room?" said one of the two young men who had joined Bland and Green. "There are plenty in the house. I'll see."

And away he went to the bar.

"Come," he said, returning in a few minutes; and the party followed a waiter up stairs, and were shown into a small room, neatly furnished, though smelling villanously of stale cigar smoke.

"This is cosy," was the approving remark of Bland, as they entered. Hats and overcoats were laid aside, and they drew around a table that stood in the centre of the room under the gaslight. A few passages were read from Shakspeare, then drink was ordered by one of the the party. The reading interspersed with critical comments, was again resumed; but the reading soon gave way entire to the comments, which, in a little while, passed from the text of Shakspeare to actors, actresses, prima donnas, and ballet-dancers, the relative merits of which were knowingly discussed for some time. In the midst of this discussion, oysters, in two or three styles, and a smoking dish of terrapin, ordered by a member of the company - which our young friend Green did not know - were brought in, followed by a liberal supply of wine and brandy. Bland expressed surprise, but accepted the entertainment as quite agreeable to himself.

After the supper, cigars were introduced, and after the cigars, cards. A few games were played for shilling stakes. Green, under the influence of more liquor than his head could bear, and in the midst of companions whose sphere he could not, in consequence, resist, yielded in a new direction for him. Of gambling he had always entertained a virtuous disapproval; yet, ere aware of the direction in which he was drifting, he was staking money at cards, the sums gradually increasing, until from shillings the ventures increased to dollars. Sometimes he won, and sometimes he lost; the winnings stimulating to new trials in the hope of further success, and the losses stimulating to new trials in order to recover, if possible; but, steadily, the tide, for all these little eddies of success, bore him downwards, and losses increased from single dollars to fives, and from fives to tens, his pleasant friend, Bland, supplying whatever he wanted in the most disinterested way, until an aggregate loss of nearly a hundred and fifty dollars sobered and appalled him.

The salary of Martin Green was only four hundred dollars, every cent of which was expended as fast as earned. A loss of a hundred and fifty dollars was, therefore, a serious and embarrassing matter.

"I'll call and see you to-morrow, when we can arrange this little matter," said Mr. Bland, "on parting with Green at his own door. He spoke pleasantly, but with something in his voice that chilled the nerves of his victim. On the next day while Green stood at his desk, trying to fix his mind upon his work, and do it correctly, his employer said, -

"Martin, there's a young man in the store who has asked for you."

Green turned and saw the last man on the earth he desired to meet. His pleasant friend of the evening before had called to "arrange that little matter."

"Not too soon for you, I hope," remarked Bland, with his courteous, yet now serious, smile, as he took the victim's hand.

"Yes, you *are*, too soon," was soberly answered.

The smile faded off of Bland's face.

"When will you arrange it?"

"In a few days."

"But I want the money to-day. It was a simple loan, you know."

"I am aware of that, but the amount is larger than I can manage at once," said Green.

"Can I have a part to-day?"

"Not to-day."

"To-morrow, then?"

"I'll do the best in my power."

"Very well. To-morrow, at this time, I will call. Make up the whole sum if possible, for I want it badly."

"Do you know that young man?" asked Mr. Phillips, the employer of Green, as the latter came back to his desk. The face of Mr. Phillips was unusually serious.

"His name is Bland."

"Why has he called to see you?" The eyes of Mr. Phillips were fixed intently on his clerk.

"He merely dropped in. I have met him a few times in company."

"Don't you know his character?"

"I never heard a word against him," said Green.

"Why, Martin!" replied Mr. Phillips, "he has the reputation of being one of the worst young men in our city; a base gambler's stool-pigeon, some say."

"I am glad to know it, sir," Martin had the presence of mind, in the painful confusion that overwhelmed him, to say, "and shall treat him accordingly." He went back to his desk, and resumed his work.

It is the easiest thing in the world to go to astray, but always difficult to return, Martin Green was astray, but how was he to get into the right path again? A barrier that seemed impassable was now lying across the way over which he had passed, a little while before, with lightest footsteps. Alone and unaided, he could not safely get back. The evil spirits that lure a man from virtue never counsel aright when to seek to return.

They magnify the perils that beset the road by which alone is safety, and suggest other ways that lead into labyrinths of evil from which escape is sometimes impossible. These spirits were now at the ear of our unhappy young friend, suggesting methods of relief in his embarrassing position.

If Bland were indeed such a character as Mr. Phillips had represented him, it would be ruin, in his employer's estimation, to have him call again and again for his debt. But how was he to liquidate that debt? There was nothing due him on account of salary, and there was not a friend or acquaintance to whom he could apply with any hope of borrowing.

"Man's extremity is the devil's opportunity." It was so in the present case, Green had a number of collections to make on that day, and his evil counsellors suggested his holding back the return of two of these, amounting to his indebtedness, and say that the parties were not yet ready to settle their bills. This would enable him to get rid of Bland, and gain time. So, acting upon the bad suggestion, he made up his return of collections, omitting the two accounts to which we have referred.

Now it so happened that one of the persons against whom these accounts stood, met Mr. Phillips as he was returning from dinner in the afternoon, and said to him,

"I settled that bill of yours to-day."

"That's right. I wish all my customers were as punctual," answered Mr. Phillips.

"I gave your young man a check for a hundred and five dollars."

"Thank you."

And the two men passed their respective ways.

On Mr. Phillips's return to his store, Martin rendered his account of collections, and, to the surprise of his employer, omitted the one in regard to which he had just been notified.

"Is this all?" he asked, in a tone that sent a thrill of alarm to the guilty heart of his clerk.

"Yes, sir," was the not clearly outspoken answer.

"Didn't Garland pay?"

"N-n-o, sir!" The suddenness of this question so confounded Martin, that he could not answer without a betraying hesitation.

"Martin!" Astonishment, rebuke, and accusation were in the voice of Mr. Phillips as he pronounced his clerk's name. Martin's face flushed deeply, and then grew very pale. He stood the image of guilt and fear for some moments, then, drawing out his pocket book, he brought therefrom a small roll of bank bills, and a memorandum slip of paper.

"I made these collections also." And he gave the money and memorandum to Mr. Phillips.

"A hundred and fifty dollars withheld! Martin! Martin! what *does* this mean?"

"Heaven is my witness, sir," answered the young man, with quivering lips, "that I have never wronged you out of a dollar, and had no intention of wronging you now. But I am in a fearful strait. My feet have become suddenly mired, and this was a desperate struggle for extrication - a temporary expedient only, not a premeditated wrong against you."

"Sit down, Martin," said Mr. Phillips, in a grave, but not severe, tone of voice. "Let me understand the case from first to last. Conceal nothing, if you wish to have me for a friend."

Thus enjoined, Martin told his humiliating story.

"If you had not gone into the way of temptation, the betrayer had not found you," was the remark of Mr. Phillips, when the young man ended his confession. "Do you frequent these eating and drinking saloons?"

"I go occasionally, sir."

"They are neither safe nor reputable, Martin. A young man who frequents them must have the fine tone of his manhood dimmed. There is an atmosphere of impurity about these places. Have you a younger brother?"

"Yes, sir."

"Would you think it good for him, as he emerged from youth to manhood, to visit refectories and billiard saloons?"

"No, sir, I would do all in my power to prevent it."

"Why?"

"There's danger in them, sir."

"And, knowing this, you went into the way of danger, and have fallen!"

Martin dropped his eyes to the floor in confusion.

"Bland is a stool-pigeon and you were betrayed."

"What am I to do?" asked the troubled young man. "I am in debt to him."

"He will be here to-morrow."

"Yes, sir."

"I will have a policeman ready to receive him."

"O, no, no, Sir. Pray don't do that!" answered Martin, with a distressed look.

"Why not?" demanded Mr. Phillips.

"It will ruin me."

"How?"

"Bland will denounce me."

"Let him."

"I shall be exposed to the policeman."

"An evil, but a mild one, compared with that to which you were rushing in order to disentangle yourself. I must have my way, sir. This matter has assumed a serious aspect. You are in my power, and must submit."

On the next day, punctual to the hour, Bland called.

"This is your man," said Mr. Phillips to his clerk. "Ask him into the counting-room." Bland, thus invited, walked back. As he entered, Mr. Phillips said, -

"My clerk owes you a hundred and fifty dollars, I understand."

"Yes, sir;" and the villain bowed.

"Make him out a receipt," said Mr. Phillips.

"When I receive the money," was coldly and resolutely answered. Martin glanced sideways at the face of Bland, and the sudden change in its expression chilled him. The mild, pleasant, virtuous aspect he could so well assume was gone, and he looked more like a fiend than a man. In pictures he had seen eyes such as now gleamed on Mr. Phillips, but never in a living face before.

The officer, who had been sitting with a newspaper in his hand, now gave his paper a quick rattle as he threw it aside, and, coming forward, stood beside Mr. Phillips, and looked steadily at the face of Bland, over which passed another change: it was less assured, but not less malignant.

Mr. Phillips took out his pocket-book, and, laying a twenty-dollar bill on the desk by which they were standing, said, -

"Take this and sign a receipt."

"No, sir!" was given with determined emphasis. "I am

not to be robbed in this way!"

"Ned," the officer now spoke, "take my advice, and sign a receipt."

"It's a cursed swindle!" exclaimed the baffled villain.

"We will dispense with hard names, sir!" The officer addressed him sternly. "Either take the money, or go. This is not a meeting for parley. I understand you and your operations."

A few moments Bland stood, with an irresolute air; then, clutching desperately at a pen, he dashed off a receipt, and was reaching for the money, when Mr. Phillips drew it back, saying, -

"Wait a moment, until I examine the receipt." He read it over, and then, pushing it towards Bland, said, -

"Write 'In full of all demands.'" A growl was the oral response. Bland took the pen again, and wrote as directed.

"Take my advice, young man, and adopt a safer and more honorable business," said Mr. Phillips, as he gave him the twenty-dollar bill.

"Keep your advice for them that ask it!" was flung back in his face. A look of hate and revenge burned in the fellow's eyes. After glaring at Mr. Phillips and Martin in a threatening way for several moments, he left more hurriedly than he had entered.

"And take my advice," said the officer, laying his hand on Martin's arm, - he spoke in a warning tone, - "and keep out of that man's way. He'll never forgive you. I know him and his prowling gang, and they are a set of as hardened and dangerous villains as can be found in the city. You are 'spotted' by them from this day, and they number a dozen at least. So, if you would be safe, avoid their haunts. Give drinking saloons and billiard rooms a wide berth. One experience like this should last you a life-time."

Thus Martin escaped from his dangerous entanglement, but never again to hold the unwavering confidence of his employer. Mr. Phillips pitied, but could not trust him fully. A year afterwards came troublesome times, losses in business, and depression in trade. Every man had to retrench. Thousands of clerks lost their places, and anxiety and distress were on every hand. Mr. Phillips, like others, had to reduce expenses, and, in reducing, the lot to go fell upon Martin Green. He had been very circumspect, had kept away from the old places where danger lurked, had devoted himself with renewed assiduity to his employer's interests; but, for all this, doubts were forever arising in the mind of Mr. Phillips, and when the question, "Who shall go?" came up, the decision was against Martin. We pity him, but cannot blame his employer.

III

ANDY LOVELL

ALL the village was getting out with Andy Lovell, the shoemaker; and yet Andy Lovell's shoes fitted so neatly, and wore so long, that the village people could ill afford to break with him. The work made by Tompkins was strong enough, but Tompkins was no artist in leather. Lyon's fit was good, and his shoes neat in appearance, but they had no wear in them. So Andy Lovell had the run of work, and in a few years laid by enough to make him feel independent. Now this feeling of independence is differently based with different men. Some must have hundreds of thousands of dollars for it to rest upon, while others find tens of thousands sufficient. A few drop below the tens, and count by units. Of this last number was Andy Lovell, the shoemaker.

When Andy opened his shop and set up business for himself, he was twenty-four years of age. Previous to that time he had worked as journeyman, earning good wages, and spending as fast as he earned, for he had no particular love of money, nor was he ambitious to rise and make an appearance in the world. But it happened with Andy as with most young men he fell in love; and as the village beauty was compliant, betrothal followed. From this time he was changed in many things, but most of all in his regard for money. From a free-handed young man, he became prudent and saving, and in a single year laid by enough to warrant setting up business for himself. The wedding followed soon after.

The possession of a wife and children gives to most men broader views of life. They look with more earnestness into the future, and calculate more narrowly the chances of success. In the ten years that followed Andy Lovell's marriage no one could have given more attention to business, or devoted more thought and care to the pleasure of customers. He was ambitious to lay up money for his wife's and children's sake, as well as to secure for himself the means of rest from labor in his more advancing years. The consequence was, that Andy served his neighbors, in his vocation, to their highest satisfaction. He was useful, contented, and thrifty.

A sad thing happened to Andy and his wife after this. Scarlet fever raged in the village one winter, sweeping many little ones into the grave. Of their three children, two were taken; and the third was spared, only to droop, like a frost-touched plant, and die ere the summer came. From that time, all of Andy Lovell's customers noted a change in the man; and no wonder. Andy had loved these children deeply. His thought had all the while been running into the future, and building castles for them to dwell in. Now the future was as nothing to him; and so his heart beat feebly in the present. He had already accumulated enough for himself and his wife to live on for the rest of their days; and, if no more children came, what motive was there for a man of his views and temperament to devote himself, with the old ardor, to business?

So the change noticed by his customers continued. He was less anxious to accommodate; disappointed them oftener; and grew impatient under complaint or remonstrance. Customers, getting discouraged or offended, dropped away, but it gave Andy no concern. He had, no longer, any heart in his business; and worked in it more like an automaton than a live human being.

At last, Andy suddenly made up his mind to shut up his shop, and retire from business. He had saved enough to live on - why should he go on any longer in this halting, miserable way - a public servant, yet pleasing nobody?

Mrs. Lovell hardly knew what to say in answer to her husband's suddenly formed resolution. It was as he alleged; they had laid up sufficient; to make them comfortable for the rest of their lives; and, sure enough, why should Andy worry himself any longer with the shop? As far as her poor reason went, Mrs. Lovell had nothing to oppose; but all her instincts were on the other side - she could not feel that it would be right.

But Andy, when he made up his mind to a thing, was what people call hard-headed. His "I won't stand it any longer," meant more than this common form of speech on the lips of ordinary men. So he gave it out that he should quit business; and it was soon all over the village. Of course Tompkins and Lyon were well enough pleased, but there were a great many who heard of the shoemaker's determination with regret. In the face of all difficulties and annoyances, they had continued to depend on him for foot garniture, and were now haunted by unpleasant images of cramped toes, corns, bunyons, and all the varied ill attendant on badly made and badly fitting shoes, boots, and gaiters. The retirement of Andy, cross and unaccommodating as he had become, was felt, in many homes, to be a public calamity.

"Don't think of such a thing, Mr. Lovell," said one.

"We can't do without you," asserted another.

"You'll not give up altogether," pleaded a third, almost coaxingly.

But Andy Lovell was tired of working without any heart in his work; and more tired of the constant fret and worry attendant upon a business in which his mind had ceased to feel interest. So he kept to his resolution, and went on with his arrangements for closing the shop.

"What are you going to do?" asked a neighbor.

"Do?" Andy looked, in some surprise, at his interrogator.

"Yes. What are you going to do? A man in good health, at your time of life, can't be idle. Rust will eat him up."

"Rust?" Andy looked slightly bewildered.

"What's this?" asked the neighbor, taking something from Andy's counter.

"An old knife," was the reply. "It dropped out of the window two or three months ago and was lost. I picked it up this morning."

"It's in a sorry condition," said the neighbor. "Half eaten up with rust, and good for nothing."

"And yet," replied the shoemaker, "there was better stuff in that knife, before it was lost, than in any other knife in the shop."

"Better than in this?" And the neighbor lifted a clean, sharp-edged knife from Andy's cutting-board.

"Worth two of it."

"Which knife is oldest?" asked the neighbor.

"I bought them at the same time."

"And this has been in constant use?"

"Yes."

"While the other lay idle, and exposed to the rains and dews?"

"And so has become rusted and good for nothing. Andy, my friend, just so rusted, and good for nothing as a man, are you in danger of becoming. Don't quit business; don't fall out of your place; don't pass from useful work into self-corroding idleness, You'll be miserable - miserable."

The pertinence of this illustration struck the mind of Andy Lovell, and set him to thinking; and the more he thought, the more disturbed became his mental state. He had, as we have see, no longer any heart in his business. All that he desired was obtained - enough to live on comfortably; why, then, should he trouble himself with hard-to-please and ill-natured customers? This was one side of the question.

The rusty knife suggested the other side. So there was conflict in his mind; but only a disturbing conflict. Reason acted too feebly on the side of these new-coming convictions. A desire to be at once, and to escape daily work and daily troubles, was stronger than any cold judgement of the case.

"I'll find something to do," he said, within himself, and so pushed aside unpleasantly intruding thoughts. But Mrs. Lovell did not fail to observe, that since, her husband's determination to go out of business, he had become more irritable than before, and less at ease in every way.

The closing day came at last. Andy Lovell shut the blinds before the windows of his shop, at night-fall, saying, as he did so, but in a half-hearted, depressed kind of a way, "For the last time;" and then going inside, sat down in front of the counter, feeling strangely and ill at ease. The future looked very blank. There was nothing in it to strive for, to hope for, to live for. Andy was no philosopher. He could not reason from any deep knowledge of human nature. His life had been merely sensational, touching scarcely the confines of interior thought. Now he felt that he was getting adrift, but could not understand the why and the wherefore.

As the twilight deepened, his mental obscurity deepened also. He was still sitting in front of his counter, when a form darkened his open door. It was the postman, with a letter for Andy's wife. Then he closed the door, saying in his thought, as he had said when closing the shutters, "For the last time," and went back into the house with the letter in his hand. It was sealed with black. Mrs. Lovell looked frightened as she noticed this sign of death. The contents were soon known. An only sister, a widow, had died suddenly, and this letter announced the fact. She left three young children, two girls and a boy. These, the letter stated, had been dispensed among the late husband's relatives; and there was a sentence or two expressing a regret that they should be separated from each other.

Mrs. Lovell was deeply afflicted by this news, and abandoned herself, for a while, to excessive grief. Her husband had no consolation to offer, and so remained, for the evening, silent and thoughtful. Andy Lovell did not sleep well that night. Certain things were suggested to his mind, and dwelt upon, in spite of many efforts to thrust them aside. Mrs. Lovell was wakeful also, as was evident to her husband from her occasional sighs, sobs, and restless movements; but no words passed between them. Both rose earlier than usual.

Had Andy Lovell forgotten that he opened his shop door, and put back the shutters, as usual? Was this mere habit-work, to be corrected when he bethought himself of what he had done? Judging from his sober face and deliberate manner - no. His air was not that of a man acting unconsciously.

Absorbed in her grief, and troubled with thoughts of her sister's oprhaned children, Mrs. Lovell did not, at first, regard the opening of her husband's shop as anything unusual. But, the truth flashing across her mind, she went in where Lovell stood at his old place by the cutting-board, on which was laid a side of morocco, and said, -

"Why, Andy! I thought you had shut up the shop for good and all."

"I thought so last night, but I've changed my mind," was the low-spoken but decided answer.

"Changed your mind! Why?"

"I don't know what you may think about it, Sally; but my mind's made up." And Andy squared round, and looked steadily into his wife's face. "There's just one thing we've got to do; and it's no use trying to run away from it. That letter didn't come for nothing. The fact is, Sally, them children mustn't be separated. I've been thinking about it all night, and it hurts me dreadfully."

"How can we help it? Mary's dead, and her husband's relations have divided the children round. I've no doubt they will be well cared for," said Mrs. Lovell.

She had been thinking as well as her husband, but not to so clear a result. To bring three little children into her quiet home, and accept years of care, of work, of anxiety, and responsibility, was not a thing to be done on light consideration. She had turned from the thought as soon as presented, and pushed it away from every avenue through which it sought to find entrance. So she had passed the wakeful night, trying to convince herself that her dead sister's children would be happy and well cared for.

"If they are here, Sally, we can be certain that they are well cared for," replied Andy.

"O, dear! I can never undertake the management of three children!" said Mrs. Lovell, her countenance expressing the painful reluctance she felt.

Andy turned partly away from his wife, and bent over the cutting-board. She saw, as he did so, an expression of countenance that rebuked her.

"A matter like this should be well considered," remarked Mrs. Lovell.

"That's true," answered her husband. "So take your time. They're your flesh and blood, you know, and if they come here, you'll have the largest share of trouble with them."

Mrs. Lovell went back into the house to think alone, while Andy commenced cutting out work, his hands moving with the springs of a readier will than had acted through them for a long time.

It took Mrs. Lovell three or four days to make up her mind to send for the children, but the right decision came at last. All this while Andy was busy in his shop - cheerfully at work, and treating the customers, who, hearing that he had changed his mind, were pressing in upon him with their orders, much after the pleasant fashion in which he had treated them in years gone by. He knew that his wife would send for the children; and after their arrival, he knew that he would have increased expenses. So, there had come a spur to action, quickening the blood in his veins; and he was at work once more, with heart and purpose, a happier man, really, than he had been for years.

Two or three weeks passed, and then the long silent

dwelling of Andy Lovell was filled with the voices of children. Two or three years have passed since then. How is it with Andy? There is not a more cheerful man in all the village, though he is in his shop early and late. No more complaints from customers. Every one is promptly and cheerfully served. He has the largest run of work, as of old; and his income is sufficient not only to meet increased expenses, but to leave a surplus at the end of every year. He is the bright, sharp knife, always in use; not the idle blade, which had so narrowly escaped, falling from the window, rusting to utter worthlessness in the dew and rain.

IV

A MYSTERY EXPLAINED

"GOING to the Falls and to the White Mountains!"

"Yes, I'm off next week."

"How long will you be absent?"

"From ten days to two weeks."

"What will it cost?"

"I shall take a hundred dollars in my pocket-book! That will carry me through."

"A hundred dollars! Where did you raise that sum? Who's the lender? Tell him he can have another customer."

"I never borrow."

"Indeed! Then you've had a legacy."

"No, and never expect to have one. All my relations are poor."

"Then unravel the mystery. Say where the hundred

dollars came from."

"The answer is easy. I saved it from my salary."

"What?"

"I saved it during the last six months for just this purpose, and now I am to have two weeks of pleasure and profit combined."

"Impossible!"

"I have given you the fact."

"What is your salary, pray?"

"Six hundred a year."

"So I thought. But you don't mean to say that in six months you have saved one hundred dollars out of three hundred?"

"Yes; that is just what I mean to say."

"Preposterous. I get six hundred, and am in debt."

"No wonder."

"Why no wonder?"

"If a man spends more than he receives, he will fall in debt."

"Of course he will. But on a salary of six hundred, how is it possible for a man to keep out of debt?"

"By spending less than he receives."

"That is easily said."

"And as easily done. All that is wanted is prudent forethought, integrity of purpose, and self-denial. He must take care of the pennies, and the pounds will take care of themselves."

"Trite and obsolete."

"True if trite; and never obsolete. It is as good doctrine to-day as it was in poor Richard's time. Of that I can bear witness."

"I could never be a miser or a skinflint."

"Nor I. But I can refuse to waste my money in unconsidered trifles, and so keep it for more important things; for a trip to Niagara and the White Mountains, for instance."

The two young men who thus talked were clerks, each receiving the salary already mentioned - six hundred dollars. One of them, named Hamilton, understood the use of money; the other, named Hoffman, practised the abuse of this important article. The consequence was, that while Hamilton had a hundred dollars saved for a trip during his summer vacation, Hoffman was in debt for more than two or three times that amount.

The incredulous surprise expressed by Hoffman was sincere. He could not understand the strange fact which had been announced. For an instant it crossed his mind that Hamilton might only have advanced his seeming impossible economy as a cover to dishonest practices.

But he pushed the thought away as wrong.

"Not much room for waste of money on a salary of six hundred a year," answered Hoffman.

"There is always room for waste," said Hamilton. "A leak is a leak, be it ever so small. The quart flagon will as surely waste its precious contents through a fracture that loses only a drop at a time, as the butt from which a constant stream is pouring. The fact is, as things are in our day, whether flagon or butt, leakage is the rule not the exception."

"I should like to know where the leak in my flagon is to be found," said Hoffman. "I think it would puzzle a finance committee to discover it."

"Shall I unravel for you the mystery?"

"You unravel it! What do you know of my affairs?"

"I have eyes."

"Do I waste my money?"

"Yes, if you have not saved as much as I have during the last six months; and yes, if my eyes have given a true report."

"What have your eyes reported?"

"A system of waste, in trifles, that does not add anything substantial to your happiness and certainly lays the foundation for a vast amount of disquietude, and almost certain embarrassment in money affairs, and consequent humiliations."

Hoffman shook his head gravely answering, "I can't see it."

"Would you like to see it?"

"O, certainly, if it exists."

"Well, suppose we go down into the matter of expenditures, item by item, and make some use of the common rules of arithmetic as we go along. Your salary, to start with, is six hundred dollars, and you play the same as I do for boarding and washing, that is, four and a half dollars per week, which gives the sum of two hundred and thirty-four dollars a year. What do your clothes cost?"

"A hundred and fifty dollars will cover everything!"

"Then you have two hundred and sixteen dollars left. What becomes of that large sum?"

Hoffman dropped his eyes and went to thinking. Yes, what had become of these two hundred and sixteen dollars? Here was the whole thing in a nutshell.

"Cigars," said Hamilton. "How many do you use in a day?"

"Not over three. But these are a part of considered expenses. I am not going to do without cigars."

"I am only getting down to the items," answered the friend. "We must find out where the money goes. Three cigars a day, and, on an average, one to a friend, which makes four."

"Very well, say four."

"At six cents apiece."

Hamilton took a slip of paper and made a few figures.

"Four cigars a day at six cents each, cost twenty-four cents. Three hundred and sixty-five by twenty-four gives eighty-seven dollars and sixty cents, as the cost of your cigars for a year."

"O, no! That is impossible," returned Hoffman, quickly.

"There is the calculation. Look at it for yourself," replied Hamilton, offering the slip of paper.

"True as I live!" ejaculated the other, in unfeigned surprise. "I never dreamed of such a thing. Eighty-seven dollars. That will never do in the world. I must cut this down."

"A simple matter of figures. I wonder you had not thought of counting the cost. Now I do not smoke at all. It is a bad habit, that injures the health, and makes us disagreeable to our friends, to say nothing of the expense. So you see how natural the result, that at the end of the year I should have eighty-seven dollars in band, while you had puffed away an equal sum in smoke. So much for the cigar account. I think you take a game of billiards now and then."

"Certainly I do. Billiards are innocent. I am very fond of the game, and must have some recreation."

"Exactly so. The question now is, What do they cost?"

"Nothing to speak of. You can't make out a case here."

"We shall see. How often do you play?"

"Two or three times a week."

"Say twice a week."

"Yes."

"Very well. Let it be twice. A shilling a game must be paid for use of the table?"

"Which comes from the loser's pocket. I, generally, make it a point to win."

"But lose sometimes."

"Of course. The winning is rarely all on one side."

"One or two games a night?"

"Sometimes."

"Suppose we put down an average loss of three games in a week. Will that be too high?"

"No. Call it three games a week."

"Or, as to expense. three shillings. Then, after the play, there comes a glass of ale - or, it may be oysters."

"Usually."

"Will two shillings at week, taking one week with another, pay for your ale and oysters?"

Hoffman did not answer until he had reflected for a few moments, Then he said, -

"I'm afraid neither two nor four shillings will cover this item. We must set it down at six."

"Which gives for billiards, ale and oysters, the sum of one dollar and a shilling per week. Fifty-two by a dollar twelve-and-a-half, and we have the sum of fifty-eight dollars and fifty cents. Rather a serious item this, in the year's expense, where the income is only six hundred dollars!"

Hoffman looked at his friend in a bewildered kind of way. This was astounding.

"How often do you go to the theatre and opera?" Hamilton went on with his questions.

"Sometimes once a week. Sometimes twice or thrice, according to the attraction."

"And you take a lady now and then?"

"Yes."

"Particularly during the opera season?"

"Yes. I'm not so selfish as always to indulge in these pleasures alone."

"Very well. Now for the cost. Sometimes the opera is one dollar. So it costs two dollars when you take a lady."

"Which is not very often."

"Will fifty cents a week, averaging the year, meet this expense?"

After thinking for some time, Hoffman said yes, he thought that fifty cents a week would be a fair appropriations.

"Which adds another item of twenty-six dollars a year to your expenses."

"But would you cut off everything?" objected Hoffman. "Is a man to have no recreations, no amusements?"

"That is another question," coolly answered Hamilton. "Our present business is to ascertain what has become of the two hundred and sixteen dollars which remained of your salary after boarding and clothing bills were paid. That is a handsome gold chain. What did it cost?"

"Eighteen dollars."

"Bought lately?"

"Within six months."

"So much more accounted for. Is that a diamond pin?"

Hoffman colored a little as he answered, -

"Not a very costly one. Merely a scarf-pin, as you. see. Small, though brilliant. Always worth what I paid for it."

"Cost twenty-five or thirty dollars?"

"Twenty-five."

"Shall I put that down as one of the year expenses?"

"Yes, you may do so."

"What about stage and car hire? Do you ride or walk to and from business?"

"I ride, of course. You wouldn't expect me to walk nearly a mile four times a day."

"I never ride, except in bad weather. The walk gives me just the exercise I need. Every man, who is confined in a store or counting-room during business hours, should walk at least four miles a day. Taken in installments of one mile at a time, at good intervals, there is surely no hardship in this exercise. Four rides, at six-pence a ride and we have another item of twenty-five cents at day. You go down town nearly every evening?"

"Yes."

"And ride both ways?

"Yes."

"A shilling more, or thirty seven and a half cents daily for car and stage hire. Now for another little calculation. Three hundred days, at three shillings a day. There it is."

And Hamilton reached a slip of paper to his friend.

"Impossible!" The latter actually started to his feet. "A

hundred and twelve dollars and fifty cents!"

"If you spend three shillings a day, you will spend that sum in a year. Figures are inexorable."

Hoffman sat down again in troubled surprise, saying,

"Have you got to the end?"

"Not yet," replied his companion.

"Very well. Go on."

"I often notice you with candies, or other confections; and you are, sometimes, quite free in sharing them with your friends. Burnt almonds, sugar almonds, Jim Crow's candied fruits, macaroons, etc. These are not to be had for nothing; and besides their cost they are a positive injury to the stomach. You, of course, know to what extent you indulge this weakness of appetite. Shall we say that it costs an average of ten cents a day?"

"Add fruit, in and out of season, and call it fifteen cents," replied Hoffman.

"Very well. For three hundred days this will give another large sum - forty-five dollars?"

"Anything more?" said Hoffman in a subdued, helpless kind of way, like one lying prostrate from a sudden blow.

"I've seen you driving out occasionally; sometimes on Sunday. And, by the way, I think you generally take an excursion on Sunday. over to Staten Island, or to

Hoboken, or up the river, or - but no matter where; you go about and spend money on the Sabbath day. How much does all this cost? A dollar a week? Seventy-five cents? Fifty cents? We are after the exact figures as near as maybe. What does it cost for drives and excursions, and their spice of refreshment?"

"Say thirty dollars a year."

"Thirty dollars, then, we will call it. And here let us close, in order to review the ground over which we have been travelling. All those various expenses, not one of which is for things essential to health, comfort, or happiness, but rather for their destruction, amount to the annual sum of four hundred and two dollars sixty cents, - you can go over the figures for yourself. Add to this three hundred and eighty-four dollars, the cost of boarding and clothing, and you swell the aggregate to nearly eight hundred dollars; and your salary is but six hundred!"

A long silence followed.

"I am amazed, confounded!" said Hoffman, resting his head between his hands, as he leaned on the table at which they were sitting. "And not only amazed and confounded," he went on, "but humiliated, ashamed! Was I a blind fool that I did not see it myself? Had I forgotten my multiplication table?"

"You are like hundreds - nay, thousands," replied the friend, "to whom a sixpence, a shilling, or even a dollar spent daily has a very insignificant look; and who never stop to think that sixpence a day amounts to over twenty dollars in a year; a shilling a day to over forty; and a dollar a day to three hundred and sixty-five. We cannot waste our money in trifles, and yet have it to spend for substantial benefits. The cigars you smoked in the past year; the games of billiards you played; the ale and oysters, cakes, confections, and fruit consumed; the rides in cars and stages; the drives and Sunday excursions, crave only the briefest of pleasures, and left new and less easily satisfied desires behind. It will not do, my friend, to grant an easy indulgence to natural appetite and desire, for they ever seek to be our masters. If we would be men - self-poised, self-controlling, self-possessing men - we must let reason govern in all our actions. We must be wise, prudent, just, and self-denying; and from this rule of conduct will spring order, tranquillity of mind, success, and true enjoyment. I think, Hoffman, that I am quite as happy a man as you are; far happier, I am sure, at this moment; and yet I have denied myself nearly all theses indulgences through which you have exhausted your means and embarrassed yourself with debt. Moreover, I have a hundred dollars clear of everything, with which I shall take a long-desired excursion, while you will be compelled, for lack of the very money which has been worse than wasted, to remain a prisoner in the city. Pray, be counselled to a different course in future."

"I would be knave or fool to need further incentive," said Hoffman, with much bitterness. "At the rate I am going on, debt, humiliation, and disgrace are before me. I may live up to my income without actually wronging others - but not beyond it. As things are now going, I am two hundred dollars worse off at the end of each year when than I began, and, worse still, weaker as to moral purpose, while the animal and sensual natures, from constant indulgence, have grown stronger. I must break this thraldom now; for, a year hence, it may be too late! Thank, you, my friend, for your plain talk. Thank you for teaching me anew the multiplication table, I shall, assuredly, not forget it again."

V

WHAT CAN I DO?

HE was a poor cripple - with fingers twisted out of all useful shape, and lower limbs paralyzed so that he had to drag them after him wearily when he moved through the short distances that limited his sphere of locomotion - a poor, unhappy, murmuring, and, at times, ill-natured cripple, eating the bread which a mother's hard labor procured for him. For hours every fair day, during spring, summer, and autumn, he might be seen in front of the little house where he lived leaning upon the gate, or sitting on an old bench looking with a sober face at the romping village children, or dreamily regarding the passengers who moved with such strong limbs up and down the street. How often, bitter envy stung the poor cripple's heart! How often, as the thoughtless village children taunted him cruelly with his misfortune, would he fling harsh maledictions after them. Many pitied the poor cripple; many looked upon him with feelings of disgust and repulsion; but few, if any, sought to do him good.

Not far from where the cripple lived was a man who had been bedridden for years, and who was likely to remain so to the end of his days. He was supported by the patient industry of a wife.

"If good works are the only passport to heaven," he said to a neighbor one day, "I fear my chances will be small."

"'Well done, good and faithful servant,' is the language of welcome," was replied; and the neighbor looked at the sick man in a way that made him feel a little uncomfortable.

"I am sick and bedridden - what can I do?" he spoke, fretfully.

"When little is given, little is required. But if there be only a single talent it must be improved."

"I have no talent," said the invalid.

"Are you sure of that?"

"What can I do? Look at me! No health, no strength, no power to rise from this bed. A poor, helpless creature, burdening my wife. Better for me, and for all, if I were in my grave."

"If that were so you would be in your grave. But God knows best. There is something for you to do, or you would be no longer permitted to live," said the neighbor.

The sick man shook his head.

"As I came along just now," continued the neighbor, "I stopped to say a word to poor Tom Hicks, the cripple, as he stood swinging on the gate before his mother's house, looking so unhappy that I pitied him in my heart. 'What do you do with yourself all through these long days, Tom?' I asked. 'Nothing,' he replied, moodily. 'Don't you read sometimes?' I queried. 'Can't read,' was his sullen answer. 'Were you never at school?' I went on. 'No: how can I get to school?' 'Why don't your mother teach you?' 'Because she can't read herself,' replied Tom. 'It isn't too late to begin now,' said I, encouragingly; 'suppose I were to find some one willing to teach you, what would you say?' The poor lad's face brightened as if the sunshine had fallen upon it; and he answered, 'I would say that nothing could please me better.' I promised to find him a teacher; and, as I promised, the thought of you, friend Croft, came into my mind. Now, here is something that you can do; a good work in which you can employ your one talent."

The sick man did not respond warmly to this proposition. He had been so long a mere recipient of good offices, - had so long felt himself the object towards which pity and service must tend, - that he had nearly lost the relish for good deeds. Idle dependence had made him selfish.

"Give this poor cripple a lesson every day," went on the neighbor, pressing home the subject, "and talk and read to him. Take him in charge as one of God's children, who needs to be instructed and led up to a higher life than the one he is now living. Is not this a good and a great work? It is, my friend, one that God has brought to your hand, and in the doing of which there will be great reward. What can you do? Much! Think of that poor boy's weary life, and of the sadder years that lie still before him. What will become of him when his mother dies? The almshouse alone will open its doors for the helpless one. But who can tell what resources may open before him if stimulated by thought. Take him, then, and unlock the doors of a mind that now sits in darkness, that sunlight may come in. To you it will give a few hours of pleasant work each day; to him it will be a life-long benefit. Will you do it?"

"Yes."

The sick man could not say "No," though in uttering that half-extorted assent he manifested no warm interest in the case of poor Tom Hicks.

On the next day the cripple came to the sick man, and received his first lesson; and every day, at an appointed hour, he was in Mr. Croft's room, eager for the instruction he received. Quickly he mastered the alphabet, and as quickly learned to construct small words, preparatory to combining them in a reading lesson.

After the first three or four days the sick man, who, had undertaken this work with reluctance, began to find his heart going down into it. Tom was so ready a scholar, so interested, and so grateful, that Mr. Croft found the task of instructing him a real pleasure. The neighbor, who had suggested this useful employment of the invalid's time, looked in now and then to see how matters were progressing, and to speak words of encouragement.

Poor Tom was seen less frequently than before hanging on the gate, or sitting idly on the bench before his mother's dwelling; and when you did find him there, as of old, you saw a different expression on his face. Soon the children, who had only looked at him, half in fear, from a distance, or come closer to the gate where he stood gazing with his strange eyes out into the street, in order to worry him, began to have a different feelings for the cripple, and one and another stopped occasionally to speak with him; for Tom no longer made queer faces, or looked at them wickedly, as if he would harm them if in his power, nor retorted angrily if they said things to worry him. And now it often happened that a little boy or girl, who had pitied the poor cripple, and feared him at the same time, would offer him a flower, or an apple, or at handful of nuts in passing to school; and he would take these gifts thankfully, and feel better all day in remembrance of the kindness with which they had been bestowed. Sometimes he would risk to see their books, and his eyes would run eagerly over the pages so far in advance of his comprehension, yet with the hope in his heart of one day mastering them; for he had grown all athirst for knowledge.

As soon as Tom could read, the children in the neighborhood, who had grown to like him, and always gathered around him at the gate, when they happened to find him there, supplied him with books; so that he had an abundance of mental food, and now began to repay his benefactor, the bedridden man, by reading to him for hours every day.

The mind of Tom had some of this qualities of a sponge: it absorbed a great deal, and, like a sponge, gave out freely at every pressure.

Whenever his mind came in contact with another mind, it must either absorb or impart. So he was always talking or always listening when he had anybody who would talk or listen.

There was something about him that strongly attracted the boys in the neighborhood, and he usually had three or four of them around him and often a dozen, late in the afternoon, when the schools were out. As Tom had entered a new world, - the world of books, - and was interested in all he found there, the subjects on which he talked with the boys who sought his company were always instructive. There, was no nonsense about the cripple: suffering of body and mind had long ago made him serious; and all nonsense, or low, sensual talk, to which boys are sometimes addicted, found no encouragement in his presence. His influence over these boys was therefore of the best kind. The parents of some of the children, when they found their sons going so often to the house of Tom Hicks, felt doubts as to the safety of such intimate intercourse with the cripple, towards whom few were prepossessed, as he bore in the village the reputation of being ill-tempered and depraved, and questioned them very closely in regard to the nature of their intercourse. The report of these boys took their parents by surprise; but, on investigation, it proved to be true, and Tom's character soon rose in the public estimation.

Then came, as a natural consequence, inquiry as to the cause of such a change in the unfortunate lad; and the neighbor of the sick man who had instructed Tom told the story of Mr. Croft's agency in the matter. This interested the whole town in both the cripple and his bedridden instructor. The people were taken by surprise at such a notable interest of the great good which may sometimes be done where the means look discouragingly small. Mr. Croft was praised for his generous conduct, and not only praised, but helped by many who had, until now, felt indifferent, towards his case - for his good work rebuked them for neglected opportunities.

The cripple's eagerness to learn, and rapid progress under the most limited advantages, becoming generally known, a gentleman, whose son had been one of Tom's visitors, and who had grown to be a better boy under his influence, offered to send him in his wagon every day to the school-house, which stood half a mile distant, and have him brought back in the afternoon.

It was the happiest day in Tom's life when he was helped down from the wagon, and went hobbling into the school-room.

Before leaving home on that morning he had made his way up to the sick room of Mr. Croft.

"I owe it all to you," he said, as he brought the white, thin hand of his benefactor to his lips. It was damp with more than a kiss when he laid it back gently on the bed. "And our Father in heaven will reward you."

"You have done a good work," said the neighbor, who had urged Mr. Croft to improve his one talent, as he sat talking with him on that evening about the poor cripple and his opening prospects; "and it will serve you in that day when the record of life is opened. Not because of the work itself, but for the true charity which prompted the work. It was begun, I know, in some self-denial, but that self-denial was for another's good; and because you put away love of ease, and indifference, and forced yourself to do kind offices, seeing that it was right to help others, God will send a heavenly love of doing good into your soul, which always includes a great reward, and is the passport to eternal felicities.

"You said," continued the neighbor, "only a few months ago, 'What can I do?' and spoke as a man who felt that he was deprived of all the means of accomplishing good; and yet you have, with but little effort, lifted a human soul out of the dark valley of ignorance, where it was groping ill self-torture, and placed it on an ascending mountain path. The light of hope has fallen, through your aid, with sunny warmth upon a heart that was cold and barren a little while ago, but is now green with verdure, and blossoming in the sweet promise of fruit. The infinite years to come alone can reveal the blessings that will flow from this one act of a bedridden man, who felt that in him was no capacity for good deeds."

The advantages of a school being placed within the reach of Tom Hicks, he gave up every thought to the acquirement of knowledge. And now came a serious difficulty. His bent, stiff fingers could not be made to hold either pen or pencil in the right position, or to use them in such a way as to make intelligible signs. But Tom was too much in earnest to give up on the first, or second, or third effort. He found, after a great many trials, that he could hold a pencil more firmly than at first, and guide his hand in some obedience to his will. This was sufficient to encourage him to daily long-continued efforts, the result of which was a gradual yielding of the rigid muscles, which became in time so flexible that he could make quite passable figures, and write a fair hand. This did not satisfy him, however. He was ambitious to do better; and so kept on trying and trying, until few boys in the school could give a fairer copy.

"Have you heard the news?" said a neighbor to Mr. Croft, the poor bedridden man. It was five years from the day he gave the poor cripple, Tom Hicks, his first lesson.

"What news?" the sick man asked, in a feeble voice, not even turning his head towards the speaker. Life's pulses were running very low. The long struggle with disease was nearly over.

"Tom Hicks has received the appointment of teacher to our public school."

"Are you in earnest?" There was a mingling of surprise and doubt in the low tones that crept out upon the air.

"Yes. It is true what I say. You know that after Mr. Wilson died the directors got Tom, who was a favorite with all the scholars, to keep the school together for a few weeks until a successor could be appointed. He managed so well, kept such good order, and showed himself so capable as an instructor, that, when the election took place to-day, he received a large majority of votes over a number of highly-recommended teachers, and this without his having made application for the situation, or even dreaming of such a thing."

At this moment the cripple's well-known shuffling tread and the rattle of crutches was heard on the stairs. He came up with more than his usual hurry. Croft turned with an effort, so as to get a sight of him as he entered the room.

"I have heard the good news," he said, as he reached a hand feebly towards Tom, "and it has made my heart glad."

"I owe it all to you," replied the cripple, in a voice that

trembled with feeling. "God will reward you."

And he caught the shadowy hand, touched it with his lips, and wet it with grateful tears, as once before. Even as he held that thin, white hand the low-moving pulse took an lower beat - lower and lower - until the long-suffering heart grew still, and the freed spirit went up to its reward.

"My benefactor!" sobbed the cripple, as he stood by the wasted form shrouded in grave-clothes, and looked upon it for the last time ere the coffin-lid closed over it. "What would I have been except for you?"

Are your opportunities for doing good few, and limited in range, to all appearances, reader? Have you often said, like the bedridden man, "What can I do?" Are you poor, weak, ignorant, obscure, or even sick as he was, and shut out from contact with the busy outside world? No matter. If you have a willing heart, good work will come to your hands. Is there no poor, unhappy neglected one to whom you can speak words of encouragement, or lift out of the vale of ignorance? Think! Cast around you. You may, by a single sentence, spoken in the right time and in the right spirit, awaken thoughts in some dull mind that may grow into giant powers in after times, wielded for the world's good. While you may never be able to act directly on society to any great purpose, in consequence of mental or physical disabilities, you may, by instruction and guidance, prepare some other mind for useful work, which, but for your agency, might have wasted its powers in ignorance or crime. All around us are human souls that may be influenced. The nurse, who ministers to you in sickness, may be hurt or helped by you; the children, who look into your face and read it daily, who listen to your speech, and remember what you say, will grow better or worse, according to the spirit of your life, as it flows into them; the neglected son of a neighbor may find in you the wise counsellor who holds him back from vice. Indeed, you cannot pass a single day, whether your sphere be large or small, your place exalted or lowly, without abundant opportunities for doing good. Only the willing heart is required. As for the harvest, that is nodding, ripe for the sickle, in every man's field. What of that time when the Lord of the Harvest comes, and you bind up your sheaves and lay them at his feet?

VI

ON GUARD

"O, MAMMA! See that wicked-looking cat on the fence! She'll have one of those dear little rabbits in a minute!"

Mattie's sweet face grew pale with fear, and she trembled all over.

"It's only a picture, my dear," said Mattie's mother. "The cat can't get down, and so the rabbits are safe."

"But it looks as if she could - as if she'd jump right upon the dear little things. I wish there was a big dog, like Old Lion, there. Wouldn't he make her fly?"

"But it's only a picture. If there was a dog there, he couldn't bark nor spring at the cat."

"Why didn't the man who made the picture put in a dog somewhere, so that we could see him, and know the rabbits were safe?"

"Maybe he didn't think of it," said Mattie's mother.

"I wish he had."

"Perhaps," said the mother, "he wished to teach us this lesson, that, as there are evil and hurtful things in the world, we should never be so entirely off of our guard as the children playing, with the rabbits seem to be. Dear little things! How innocent and happy they are! There is not a thought of danger in their minds. And yet, close by them is a great cat, with cruel eyes, ready to spring upon their harmless pets. Yes; I think the artist meant to teach a lesson when he drew this picture."

"What lesson, mother?" asked Mattie. "O, I remember," she added quickly. "You said that it might be to teach us never to be off of our guard, because there are evil and hurtful things in the world."

"Yes; and that is a lesson which cannot be learned too early. Baby begins to learn it when he touches the fire and is burnt; when he pulls the cat too hard and she scratches him; when he runs too fast for his little strength, and gets a fall. And children learn it when they venture too near vicious animal and are kicked or bitten; when they tear their clothes, or get their hands and faces scratched with thorns and briers; when they fall from trees, or into the water, and in many other ways that I need not mention. And men and women learn, it very, very, often in pains and sorrows too deep for you to comprehend."

Mattie drew a long sigh, as she stood before her mother, looking, soberly into her face.

"I wish there wasn't anything bad in the world," she said. "Nothing that could hurt us."

"Ah, dear child!" answered the mother, her voice

echoing Mattie's sigh, "from millions and millions of hearts that wish comes up daily. But we have this to cheer us: if we stand on guard - if we are watchful as well as innocent - we shall rarely get hurt. It is the careless and the thoughtless that harm reaches."

"And so we must always be on guard," said Mattie, still looking very sober.

"There is no other way, my child. 'On guard' is the watchword of safety for us all, young and old. But the harm that comes from the outside is of small account compared with the, harm that comes from within."

"From within, mother! How can harm could from within?"

"You read about the 'hawk among the birds'?"

"Yes, yes - O, now I understand what you mean! Bad thoughts and feelings can do us harm."

"Yes; and the hurt is deeper and more deadly than any bodily harm, for it is done to the soul. These rabbits are like good and innocent things of the mind, and the cat like evil and cruel things. If you do not keep watch, in some unguarded moment angry passions evil arise and hurt or destroy your good affections; just as this cat, if she were real, would tear or kill the tender rabbits."

"O, mother! Is it as bad as that?" said Mattie.

"Yes, my dear; just as bad as that. And when any of these good and innocent feelings are destroyed by anger, hatred, jealousy, envy, revenge and the like, then just so much of heavenly good dies in us and just so far do we come under the power of what is evil and hurtful. Then we turn aside from safe and pleasant ways and walk among briers and thorns. Dear Mattie! consider well the lesson of this picture, and set a watch over your heart daily. But watching is not all. We are told in the Bible to pray as well as watch. All of us, young and old, must do this if we would be in safety; for human will and human effort would all be in vain to overcome evil if divine strength did not flow into them. And unless we desire and pray for this divine strength we cannot receive it."

VII

A VISIT WITH THE DOCTOR

"HOW are you to-day, Mrs. Carleton?" asked Dr. Farleigh, as he sat down by his patient, who reclined languidly in a large cushioned chair.

"Miserable," was the faintly spoken reply. And the word was repeated, - "Miserable."

The doctor took one of the lady's small, white hands, on which the network of veins, most delicately traced, spread its blue lines everywhere beneath the transparent skin. It was a beautiful hand - a study for a painter or sculptor. It was a soft, flexible hand - soft, flexible, and velvety to the touch as the hand of a baby, for it was as much a stranger to useful work. The doctor laid his fingers on the wrist. Under the pressure he felt the pulse beat slowly and evenly. He took out his watch and counted the beats, seventy in a minute. There was a no fever, nor any unusual disturbance of the system. Calmly the heart was doing its appointed work.

"How is your head, Mrs. Carleton?"

The lady moved her head from side to side two or three times.

"Anything out of the way there?"

"My head is well enough, but I feel so miserable - so weak. I haven't the strength of a child. The least exertion exhausts me."

And the lady shut her eyes, looking the picture of feebleness.

"Have you taken the tonic, for which I left a prescription yesterday?"

"Yes; but I'm no stronger."

"How is your appetite?"

"Bad."

"Have you taken the morning walk in the garden that I suggested?"

"O, dear, no! Walk out in the garden? I'm faint by the time I get to the breakfast-room! I can't live at this rate, doctor. What am I to do? Can't you build me up in some way? I'm burden to myself and every one else."

And Mrs. Carleton really looked distressed.

"You ride out every day?"

"I did until the carriage was broken, and that was nearly a week ago. It has been at the carriage-maker's ever since."

"You must have the fresh air, Mrs. Carleton," said the doctor, emphatically. "Fresh air, change of scene, and exercise, are indispensable in your case. You will die if you remain shut up after this fashion. Come, take a ride with me."

"Doctor! How absurd!" exclaimed Mrs. Carleton, almost shocked by the suggestion. "Ride with you! What would people think?"

"A fig for people's thoughts! Get your shawl and bonnet, and take a drive with me. What do you care for meddlesome people's thoughts? Come!"

The doctor knew his patient.

"But you're not in earnest, surely?" There was a half-amused twinkle in the lady's eyes.

"Never more in earnest. I'm going to see a patient just out of the city, and the drive will be a charming one. Nothing would please me better than to have your company."

There was a vein of humor, and a spirit of "don't care" in Mrs. Carleton, which had once made her independent, and almost hoydenish. But fashionable associations, since her woman-life began, had toned her down into exceeding propriety. Fashion and conventionality, however, were losing their influence, since enfeebled health kept her feet back from the world's gay places; and the doctor's invitation to a ride found her sufficiently disenthralled to see in it a pleasing novelty.

"I've half a mind to go," she said, smiling. She had not smiled before since the doctor came in.

"I'll ring for your maid," and Dr. Farleigh's hand was on the bell-rope before Mrs. Carleton had space to think twice, and endanger a change of thought.

"I'm not sure that I am strong enough for the effort," said Mrs. Carleton, and she laid her head back upon the cushions in a feeble way.

"Trust me for that," replied the doctor.

The maid came in.

"Bring me a shawl and my bonnet, Alice; I am going to ride out with the doctor." Very languidly was the sentence spoken.

"I'm afraid, doctor, it will be too much for me. You don't know how weak I am. The very thought of such an effort exhausts me."

"Not a thought of the effort," replied Dr. Farleigh. "It isn't that."

"What is it?"

"A thought of appearances - of what people will say."

"Now, doctor! You don't think me so weak in that direction?"

"Just so weak," was the free-spoken answer. "You fashionable people are all afraid of each other. You haven't a spark of individuality or true independence. No, not a spark. You are quite strong enough to ride out in your own elegant carriage but with the doctor! - O, dear, no! If you were certain of not meeting Mrs.

McFlimsey, perhaps the experiment might be adventured. But she is always out on fine days."

"Doctor, for shame! How can you say that?"

And a ghost of color crept into the face of Mrs. Carleton, while her eyes grew brighter - almost flashed.

The maid came in with shawl and bonnet. Dr. Farleigh, as we have intimated, understood his patient, and said just two or three words more, in a tone half contemptuous.

"Afraid of Mrs. McFlimsey!"

"Not I; nor of forty Mrs. McFlimseys!"

It was not the ghost of color that warmed Mrs. Carleton's face now, but the crimson of a quicker and stronger heart-beat. She actually arose from her chair without reaching for her maid's hand and stood firmly while the shawl was adjusted and the bonnet-strings tied.

"We shall have a charming ride," said the doctor, as he crowded in beside his fashionable lady companion, and took up the loose reins. He noticed that she sat up erectly, and with scarcely a sign of the languor that but a few minutes before had so oppressed her. "Lean back when you see Mrs. McFlimsey's carriage, and draw your veil closely. She'll never dream that it's you."

"I'll get angry if you play on that string much longer!" exclaimed Mrs. Carleton; "what do I care for Mrs. McFlimsey?"

How charmingly the rose tints flushed her cheeks! How the light rippled in her dark sweet eyes, that were leaden a little while before!

Away from the noisy streets, out upon the smoothly-beaten road, and amid green field and woodlands, gardens and flower-decked orchards, the doctor bore his patient, holding her all the while in pleasant talk. How different this from the listless, companionless drives taken by the lady in her own carriage - a kind of easy, vibrating machine, that quickened the sluggish blood no more than a cushioned rocking chair!

Closely the doctor observed his patient. He saw how erectly she continued to sit; how the color deepened in her face, which actually seemed rounder and fuller; how the sense of enjoyment fairly danced in her eyes.

Returning to the city by a different road, the doctor, after driving through streets entirely unfamiliar to his companion, drew up his horse before a row of mean-looking dwellings, and dropping the reins, threw open the carriage door, and stepped upon the pavement - at the same time reaching out his hand to Mrs. Carleton. But she drew back, saying, -

"What is the meaning of this, doctor?"

"I have a patient here, and I want you to see her."

"O, no; excuse me, doctor. I've no taste for such things," answered the lady.

"Come - I can't leave you alone in the carriage. Ned might take a fancy to walk off with you."

Mrs. Carleton glanced at the patient old horse, whom the doctor was slandering, with a slightly alarmed manner.

"Don't you think he'll stand, doctor?" she asked, uneasily.

"He likes to get home, like others of his tribe. Come;" and the doctor held out his hand in a persistent way.

Mrs. Carleton looked at the poor tenements before which the doctor's carriage had stopped with something of disgust and something of apprehension.

"I can never go in there, doctor."

"Why not?"

"I might take some disease."

"Never fear. More likely to find a panacea there."

The last sentence was in an undertone.

Mrs. Carleton left the carriage, and crossing the pavement, entered one of the houses, and passed up with the doctor to the second story. To his light tap at a chamber door a woman's voice said, -

"Come in."

The door was pushed open, and the doctor and Mrs. Carleton went in. The room was small, and furnished in the humblest manner, but the air was pure, and everything looked clean and tidy. In a chair, with a pillow pressed in at her back for a support, sat a pale, emaciated woman, whose large, bright eyes looked up eagerly, and in a kind of hopeful surprise, at so unexpected a visitor as the lady who came in with the doctor. On her lap a baby was sleeping, as sweet, and pure, and beautiful a baby as ever Mrs. Carleton had looked upon. The first impulse of her true woman's heart, had she yielded to it, would have prompted her to take it in her arms and cover it with kisses.

The woman was too weak to rise from her chair, but she asked Mrs. Carleton to be seated in a tone of lady-like self-possession that did not escape the visitor's observation.

"How did you pass the night, Mrs. Leslie?" asked the doctor.

"About as usual," was answered, in a calm, patient way; and she even smiled as she spoke.

"How about the pain through your side and shoulder?"

"It may have been a little easier."

"You slept?"

"Yes, sir."

"What of the night sweats?"

"I don't think they have diminished any."

The doctor beat his eyes to the floor, and sat in silence for some time. The heart of Mrs. Carleton was opening towards - the baby and it was a baby to make its way into any heart. She had forgotten her own weakness -

forgotten, in the presence of this wan and wasted mother, with a sleeping cherub on her lap, all about her own invalid state.

"I will send you a new medicine," said the doctor, looking up; then speaking to Mrs. Carleton, he added, -

"Will you sit here until I visit two or three patients in the block?"

"O, certainly," and she reached out her arms for the baby, and removed it so gently from its mother's lap that its soft slumber was not broken. When the doctor returned he noticed that there had been tears in Mrs. Carleton's eyes. She was still holding the baby, but now resigned the quiet sleeper to its mother, kissing it as she did so. He saw her look with a tender, meaning interest at the white, patient face of the sick woman, and heard her say, as she spoke a word or two in parting, -

"I shall not forget you."

"That's a sad case, doctor," remarked the lady, as she took her place in the carriage.

"It is. But she is sweet and patient."

"I saw that, and it filled me with surprise. She tells me that her husband died a year ago."

"Yes."

"And that she has supported herself by shirt-making."

"Yes."

"But that she had become too feeble for work, and is dependent on a younger sister, who earns a few dollars, weekly, at book-folding."

"The simple story, I believe," said the doctor.

Mrs. Carleton was silent for most of the way home; but thought was busy. She had seen a phase of life that touched her deeply.

"You are better for this ride," remarked the doctor, as he handed her from the carriage.

"I think so," replied Mrs. Carleton.

"There has not been so fine a color on your face for months."

They had entered Mrs. Carleton's elegant residence, and were sitting in one of her luxurious parlors.

"Shall I tell you why?" added the doctor.

Mrs. Carleton bowed.

"You have had some healthy heart-beats."

She did not answer.

"And I pray you, dear madam, let the strokes go on," continued Dr. Farleigh. "Let your mind become interested in some good work, and your hands obey your thoughts, and you will be a healthy woman, in body and soul. Your disease is mental inaction."

Mrs. Carleton looked steadily at the doctor.

"You are in earnest," she said, in a calm, firm way.

"Wholly in earnest, ma'am. I found you, an hour ago, in so weak a state that to lift your hand was an exhausting effort. You are sitting erect now, with every muscle taughtly strung. When will your carriage be home?"

He asked the closing question abruptly.

"To-morrow," was replied.

"Then I will not call for you, but -"

He hesitated.

"Say on, doctor."

"Will you take my prescription?"

"Yes." There was no hesitation.

"You must give that sick woman a ride into the country. The fresh, pure, blossom-sweet air will do her good - may, indeed, turn the balance of health in her favor. Don't be afraid of Mrs. McFlimsey."

"For shame, doctor! But you are too late in your suggestion. I'm quite ahead of you."

"Ah! in what respect?"

"That drive into the country is already a settled thing. Do you know, I'm in love with that baby?"

"Othello's occupation's gone, I see!" returned the

doctor, rising. "But I may visit you occasionally as a friend, I presume, if not as a medical adviser?"

"As my best friend, always," said Mrs. Carleton, with feeling. "You have led me out of myself, and showed me the way to health and happiness; and I have settled the question as to my future. It shall not be as the past."

And it was not.

VIII

HADN'T TIME FOR TROUBLE

MRS. CALDWELL was so unfortunate as to have a rich husband. Not that the possession of a rich husband is to be declared a misfortune, *per se*, but, considering the temperament of Mrs. Caldwell, the fact was against her happiness, and therefore is to be regarded, taking the ordinary significance, of the term, as unfortunate.

Wealth gave Mrs. Caldwell leisure for ease and luxurious self-indulgence, and she accepted the privileges of her condition. Some minds, when not under the spur, sink naturally into, a state of inertia, from which, when any touch of the spur reaches them, they spring up with signs of fretfulness. The wife and mother, no matter what her condition, who yields to this inertia, cannot escape the spur. Children and servant, excepting all other causes, will not spare the pricking heel.

Mrs. Caldwell was, by nature, a kind-hearted woman, and not lacking in good sense. But for the misfortune of having a rich husband, she might have spent an active, useful, happy life. It was the opportunity which abundance gave for idleness and ease that marred everything. Order in a household, and discipline among children, do not come spontaneously. They are the result of wise forecast, and patient, untiring, never-relaxing effort. A mere conviction of duty is rarely found to be sufficient incentive; there must be the impelling force of some strong-handed necessity. In the case of Mrs. Caldwell, this did not exist; and so she failed in the creation of that order in her family without which permanent tranquillity is impossible. In all lives are instructive episodes, and interesting as instructive. Let us take one of them from the life of this lady, whose chief misfortune was in being rich.

Mrs. Caldwell's brow was clouded. It was never, for a very long time, free from, clouds, for it seemed as if all sources of worry and vexation were on the increase; and, to make matters worse, patience was assuredly on the decline. Little things, once scarcely observed, now give sharp annoyance, there being rarely any discrimination and whether they were of accident, neglect, or wilfulness.

"Phoebe!" she called, fretfully.

The voice of her daughter answered, half-indifferently, from the next room.

"Why don't you come when I call you?" Anger now mingled with fretfulness.

The face of a girl in her seventeenth year, on which sat no very amiable expression, was presented at the door.

"Is that your opera cloak lying across the chair, and partly on the floor?"

Phoebe, without answering, crossed the room, and catching up the garment with as little carefulness as if it had been an old shawl threw it across her arm, and was retiring, when her mother said, sharply, -

"Just see how you are rumpling that cloak! What do you mean?"

"I'm not hurting the cloak, mother," answered Phoebe, coolly. Then, with a shade of reproof, she added, "You fret yourself for nothing."

"Do you call it nothing to abuse an elegant garment like that?" demanded Mrs. Caldwell. "To throw it upon the floor, and tumble it about as if it were an old rag?"

"All of which, mother mine, I have not done." And the girl tossed her head with an air of light indifference.

"Don't talk to me in that way, Phoebe! I'll not suffer it. You are forgetting yourself." The mother spoke with a sternness of manner that caused her daughter to remain silent. As they stood looking at each other, Mrs. Caldwell said, in a changed voice, -

"What is that on your front tooth?"

"A speck of something, I don't know what; I noticed it only yesterday."

Mrs. Caldwell. crossed the room hastily, with a disturbed manner, and catching hold of Phoebe's arm, drew her to a window.

"Let me see!" and she looked narrowly at the tooth, "Decay, as I live!" The last sentence was uttered in a tone of alarm. "You must go to the dentist immediately. This is dreadful! If your teeth are beginning to fail now, you'll not have one left in your head by the time you're twenty-five."

"It's only a speck," said Phoebe, evincing little concern.

"A speck! I And do you know what a speck means?" demanded Mrs. Caldwell, with no chance in the troubled expression of her face.

"What does it mean?" asked Phoebe.

"Why, it means that the quality of your teeth is not good. One speck is only the herald of another. Next week a second tooth may show signs of decay, and a third in the week afterwards. Dear - dear! This is too bad! The fact is, you are destroying your health. I've talked and talked about the way you devour candies and sweetmeats; about the way you sit up at night, and about a hundred other irregularities. There must be a change in all. This, Phoebe, as I've told you dozens and dozens of times."

Mrs. Caldwell was growing more and more excited.

"Mother! mother!" replied Phoebe, "don't fret yourself for nothing. The speck can be removed in an instant."

"But the enamel is destroyed! Don't you see that? Decay will go on."

"I don't believe that follows at all," answered Phoebe, tossing her head, indifferently, "And even if I believed in the worst, I'd find more comfort in laughing than crying." And she ran off to her own room.

Poor Mrs. Caldwell sat down to brood over this new trouble; and as she brooded, fancy wrought for her the most unpleasing images.

She saw the beauty of Phoebe, a few years later in life, most sadly marred by broken or discolored teeth. Looking at that, and that alone, it magnified itself into a calamity, grew to an evil which overshadowed everything.

She was still tormenting herself about the prospect of Phoebe's loss of teeth, when, in passing through her elegantly-furnished parlors, her eyes fell on a pale acid stain, about the size of a shilling piece, one of the rich figures in the carpet. The color of this figure was maroon, and the stain, in consequence, distinct; at least, it became very distinct to her eye as they dwelt upon it as if held there by a kind of fascination.

Indeed, for a while, Mrs. Caldwell could see nothing else but this spot on the carpet; no, not even though she turned her eyes in various directions, the retina keeping that image to the exclusion of all others.

While yet in the gall of this new bitterness, Mrs. Caldwell heard a carriage stop in front of the house, and, glancing through the window, saw that it was on the opposite side of the street. She knew it to be the carriage of a lady whose rank made her favor a desirable thing to all who were emulous of social distinction. To be of her set was a coveted honor. For her friend and neighbor opposite, Mrs. Caldwell did not feel the highest regard; and it rather hurt her to see the first call made in that quarter, instead of upon herself. It was no very agreeable thought, that this lady-queen of fashion, so much courted and regarded, might really think most highly of her neighbor opposite. To be second to her, touched the quick of pride, and hurt.

Only a card was left. Then the lady reentered her carriage. What? Driving away? Even so. Mrs. Caldwell was not even honored by a call! This was penetrating the quick. What could it mean? Was she to be ruled out of this lady's set? The thought was like a wounding arrow to her soul.

Unhappy Mrs. Caldwell! Her daughter's careless habits; the warning sign of decay among her pearly teeth; the stain on a beautiful carpet, and, worse than all as a pain-giver, this slight from a magnate of fashion; - were not these enough to cast a gloom over the state of a woman who had everything towards happiness that wealth and social station could give, but did not know how to extract from them the blessing they had power to bestow? Slowly, and with oppressed feelings, she left the parlors, and went up stairs. Half an hour later, as she sat alone, engaged in the miserable work of weaving out of the lightest material a very pall of shadows for her soul, a servant came to the door, and announced a visitor. It was an intimate friend, whom she could not refuse to see - a lady named Mrs. Bland.

"How are you, Mrs. Caldwell?" said the visitor, as the two ladies met.

"Miserable," was answered. And not even the ghost of a smile played over the unhappy face.

"Are you sick?" asked Mrs. Bland, showing some concern.

"No, not exactly sick. But, somehow or other, I'm in a worry about things all the while. I can't move a step in any direction without coming against the pricks. It seems as though all things were conspiring against me."

And then Mrs. Caldwell went, with her friend, through the whole series of her morning troubles, ending with the sentence, -

"Now, don't you think I am beset? Why, Mrs. Bland, I'm in a purgatory."

"A purgatory of your own creating, my friend," answered Mrs. Bland with the plainness of speech warranted by the intimacy of their friendship; "and my advice is to come out of it as quickly as possible."

"Come out of it! That is easily said. Will you show me the way?"

"At some other time perhaps. But this morning I have something else on hand. I've called for you to go with me on an errand of mercy."

There was no Christian response in the face of Mrs. Caldwell. She was too deep amid the gloom of her own, wretched state to have sympathy for others.

"Mary Brady is in trouble," said Mrs. Bland.

"What has happened?" Mrs. Caldwell was alive with interest in a moment.

"Her husband fell through a hatchway yesterday, and came near being killed."

"Mrs. Bland!"

"The escape was miraculous."

"Is he badly injured?"

"A leg and two ribs broken. Nothing more, I believe. But that is a very serious thing, especially where the man's labor is his family's sole dependence."

"Poor Mary!" said Mrs. Caldwell, in real sympathy. "In what a dreadful state she must be! I pity her from the bottom of my heart."

"Put on your things, and let us go and see her at once."

Now, it is never a pleasant thing for persons like Mrs. Caldwell to look other people's troubles directly in the face. It is bad enough to dwell among their own pains and annoyances, and they shrink from meddling with another's griefs. But, in the present case, Mrs. Caldwell, moved by a sense of duty and a feeling of interest in Mrs. Brady, who had, years before, been a faithful domestic in her mother's house, was, constrained to overcome all reluctance, and join her friend in the proposed visit of mercy.

"Poor Mary! What a state she must be in!"

Three or four times did Mrs. Caldwell repeat this sentence, as they walked towards that part of the town in which Mrs. Brady resided. "It makes me sick, at heart to think of it," she added.

At last they stood at the door of a small brick house, in a narrow street, and knocked. Mrs. Caldwell dreaded to enter, and even shrank a little behind her friend when she heard a hand on the lock. It was Mary who opened the door - Mary Brady, with scarcely a sign of change in her countenance, except that it was a trifle paler.

"O! Come in!" she said, a smile of pleasure brightening over her face. But Mrs. Caldwell could not smile in return. It seemed to her as if it would be a mockery of the trouble which had come down upon that humble dwelling.

"How is your husband, Mary?" she asked with a solemn face, as soon as they had entered. "I only heard a little while ago of this dreadful occurrence."

"Thank you, ma'am," replied Mrs. Brady, her countenance hardly falling to a serious tone in its expression. "He's quite comfortable to-day; and it's such a relief to see him out of pain. He suffered considerably through the night, but fell asleep just at day dawn, and slept for several hours. He awoke almost entirely free from pain."

"There are no internal injuries, I believe," said Mrs. Bland.

"None, the doctor says. And I'm so thankful. Broken bones are bad enough, and it is hard to see as kind and good a husband as I have suffer," - Mary's eyes grew wet, "but they will knit and become strong again. When I think how much worse it might have been, I am condemned for the slightest murmur that escapes my lips."

"What are you going to do, Mary?" asked Mrs. Caldwell. "Your husband won't be fit for work in a month, and you have a good many mouths to fill."

"A woman's wit and a woman's will can do a great deal," answered Mrs. Brady, cheerfully. "You see" - pointing to a table, on which lay a bundle - "that I have already been to the tailor's for work. I'm a quick sewer, and not afraid but what I can earn sufficient to keep the pot boiling until John is strong enough to go to work again. 'Where there's a will, there's a way,' Mrs. Caldwell. I've found that true so far, and I reckon it will be true to the end. John will have a good resting spell, poor man! And, dear knows, he's a right to have it, for he's worked hard, and with scarcely a holiday, since we were married."

"Well, well, Mary," said Mrs. Caldwell, in manifest surprise, "you beat me out! I can't understand it. Here you are, under circumstances that I should call of a most distressing and disheartening nature, almost as cheerful as if nothing had happened. I expected to find you overwhelmed with trouble, but, instead, you are almost as tranquil as a June day."

"The truth is," replied Mrs. Brady, drawing, almost for shame, a veil of sobriety over her face, "I've had no time to be troubled. If I'd given up, and set myself down with folded hands, no doubt I should have been miserable enough. But that isn't my way, you see. Thinking about what I shall do, and their doing it, keep me so well employed, that I don't get opportunity to look on the dark side of things. And what would be the use? There's always a bright side as well as a dark side, and I'm sure it's pleasant to be on the bright side, if we can get there; and always try to manage it, somehow."

"Your secret is worth knowing, Mary," said Mrs. Bland.

"There's no secret about it," answered the poor woman, "unless it be in always keeping busy. As I said just now, I've no time to be troubled, and so trouble, after knocking a few times at my door, and not gaining admittance, passes on to some other that stands ajar – and there are a great many such. The fact is, trouble don't like to crowd in among busy people, for they jostle her about, and never give her a quiet resting place, and so she soon departs, and creeps in among the idle ones. I can't give any better explanation, Mrs. Bland."

"Nor, may be, could the wisest philosopher that lives," returned that lady.

The two friends, after promising to furnish Mrs. Brady with an abundance of lighter and more profitable sewing than she had obtained at a clothier's, and saying and doing whatever else they felt to be best under the circumstances, departed. For the distance of a block they walked in silence. Mrs. Caldwell spoke first.

"I am rebuked," she said; "rebuked, as well as instructed. Above all places in the world, I least expected to receive a lesson there."

"Is it not worth remembering?" asked the friend.

"I wish it were engraved in ineffaceable characters on my heart. Ah, what a miserable self-tormentor I have been! The door of my heart stand always ajar, as Mary said, and trouble comes gliding in that all times, without so much as a knock to herald his coming. I must shut and bar the door!"

"Shut it, and bar it, my friend!" answered Mrs. Bland. "And when trouble knocks, say to her, that you are too busy with orderly and useful things - too earnestly at work in discharging dutiful obligations, in the larger sphere, which, by virtue of larger means, is yours to work in - to have any leisure for her poor companionship, and she will not tarry on your threshold. Throw to the winds such light causes of unhappiness as were suffered to depress you this morning, and they will be swept away like thistle down."

"Don't speak of them. My cheek burns at the remembrance," said Mrs. Caldwell.

They now stood at Mrs. Caldwell's door.

"You will come in?"

"No. The morning has passed, and I must return home."

"When shall I see you?" Mrs. Caldwell grasped tightly her friends' hand.

"In a day or two."

"Come to-morrow, and help me to learn in this new book that has been opened. I shall need a wise and a patient teacher. Come, good, true, kind friend!"

"Give yourself no time for trouble," said Mrs. Bland, with a tender, encouraging smile. "Let true thoughts and useful deeds fill all your hours. This is the first lesson. Well in the heart, and all the rest is easy."

And so, Mrs. Caldwell found it. The new life she strove to lead, was easy just in the degree she lived in the spirit of this lesson, and hard just in the degree of her departure.

IX

A GOOD NAME

TWO boys, named Jacob Peters and Ralph Gilpin were passing along Chestnut Street one evening about ten years ago, when one of them, stopped, and said, -

"Come, Ralph, let us have some oysters. I've got a quarter." They were in front of an oyster-cellar.

"No," replied Ralph, firmly. "I'm not going down there."

"I didn't mean that we should get anything to drink," replied the other.

"No matter: they sell liquor, and I don't wish to be seen in such a place."

"That's silly," said Jacob Peters, speaking with some warmth. "It can't hurt you to be seen there. They sell oysters, and all we should go there for would be to buy oysters. Come along. Don't be foolish!" And Jacob grasped the arm of Ralph, and tried to draw him towards the refectory. But Ralph stood immovable.

"What harm can it do?" asked Jacob.

"It might do at great deal of harm."

"In what way?"

"By hurting my good name."

"I don't understand you."

"I might be seen going in or coming out by some one who know me, and who might take it for granted that my visit, was for liquor."

"Well, suppose he did? He would be wrong in his inference; and what need you care? A clear conscience, I have heard my uncle say, is better than any man's opinion, good or bad."

"I prefer the clear conscience and the good opinion together, if I can secure both at the same time," said Ralph.

"O, you're too afraid of other people's opinions," replied Jacob, in a sneering manner. "As for me, I'll try to do right and be right, and not bother myself about what people may think. Come, are you going to join me in a plate of oysters?"

"No."

"Very well. Good by. I'm sorry you're afraid to do right for fear somebody may think you're going to do wrong," and Jacob Peters descended to the oyster-cellar, while Ralph Gilpin passed on his way home-ward. As Jacob entered the saloon he met a man who looked at him narrowly, and as Jacob thought, with surprise. He had seen this man before, but did not know his name.

A few weeks afterwards, the two boys, who were neighbor, sat together planning a row-boat excursion on the Schuylkill.

"We'll have Harry Elder, and Dick Jones, and Tom Forsyth," said Jacob.

"No, not Tom Forsyth," objected Ralph.

"Why not? He's a splendid rower."

"I don't wish to be seen in his company," said Ralph. "He doesn't bear a good character."

"O, well; that's nothing to us."

"I think it is a great deal to us. We are judged by the company we keep."

"Let people judge; who cares?" replied Jacob; "not I."

"Well, I do, then," answered Ralph.

"I hate to see a boy so 'fraid of a shadow as you are."

"A tainted name is no shadow; but a real evil to be afraid of."

"I don't see how our taking Tom Forsyth along is going to taint your name, or mine either."

"He's a bad boy," Ralph firmly objected. "He uses profane language. You and I have both seen him foolish from drink. And we know that he was sent home from a good place, under circumstances that threw suspicion on his honesty. This being so, I am not going to be seen in his company. I think too much of my good name."

"But, Ralph," urged Jacob, in a persuasive manner, "he's such a splendid rower. Don't be foolish about it; nobody'll see us. And we shall have such a grand time. I'll make him promise not to use a wicked word all day."

"It's no use to talk, Jacob. I'm not going in company with Tom Forsyth if I never go boating."

"You're a fool!" exclaimed Jacob, losing his temper.

Ralph's face burned with anger, but he kept back the sharp words that sprung to his lips, and after a few moments said, with forced composure, -

"There's no use in you're getting mad about it, Jacob. If you prefer Tom to me, very well. I haven't set my heart on going."

"I've spoken to Tom already" said Jacob, cooling off a little. "And he's promised to go; so there's no getting away from it. I'm sorry you're so over nice."

The rowing party came off, but Ralph was not of the number. As the boys were getting into the boat at Fairmount, Jacob noticed two or three men standing on the wharf; and on lifting his eyes to the face of one of them, he recognized the same individual who had looked at him so intently as he entered the oyster saloon. The man's eyes rested upon him for a few moments, and then turned to the boy, Tom Forsyth.

Young Peters might have been mistaken, but he thought he saw on the man's face a look of surprise and disapprobation. Somehow or other he did not feel very comfortable in mind as the boat pushed off from shore. Who was this man? and why had he looked at him twice so intently, and with something of disapproval in his face?

Jacob Peters was fifteen years old. He had left school a few weeks before, and his father was desirous of getting him into a large whole-sale house, on Market Street. A friend was acquainted with a member of the firm, and through his kind offices he hoped to make the arrangement. Some conversation had already taken place between the friend and merchant, who said they wished another lad in the store, but were very particular as to the character of their boys. The friend assured him that Jacob was a lad of excellent character; and depending on this assurance, a preliminary engagement had been made, Jacob was to go into the store just one week from the day on which he went on the boating excursion. Both his own surprise and that of his father may be imagined when a note came, saying that the firm in Market Street had changed its views in regard to a lad, and would not require the services of Jacob Peters.

The father sent back a polite note, expressing regret at the change of view, and asking that his son should still be borne in mind, as he would prefer that situation for him to any other in the city. Jacob was the bearer of this note. When he entered the store, the first person he met was the man who looked at him so closely in the oyster saloon and on the wharf at Fairmount. Jacob handed him the note, which he opened and read, and then gave him cold bow.

A glimpse of the truth passed through Jacob's mind. He had been misjudged, and here was the unhappy result. His good name had suffered, and yet he had done nothing actually wrong. But boys, like men, are judged by the company they keep and the places in which they are seen.

"I'm going into a store next week," said Ralph Gilpin, to his friend Jacob, about a week afterwards.

"Where?" asked Jacob.

"On Market Street."

"In what store?"

"In A. & L.'s," replied Ralph.

"O, no!" ejaculated Jacob, his face flushing, "not there!"

"Yes," replied Ralph. "I'm going to A. & L.'s. Father got me the place. Don't you think I'm lucky? They're very particular about the boys they taking that store. Father says he considers their choice of me quite a compliment. I'm sure I feel proud enough about it."

"Well, I think they acted very meanly," said Jacob, showing sonic anger. "They promised father that I should have the place."

"Are you sure about that?" asked the young friend.

"Certainly I am. I was to go there this week. But they sent father a note, saying they had changed their minds about a boy."

"Perhaps," suggested Ralph, "it you were seen going into a drinking saloons or in company with Tom Forsyth. You remember what I said to you about preserving a good name."

Jacob's face colored, and his eyes fell to the ground.

"O, that's only your guess," he replied, tossing his head, and putting on an incredulous look; but he felt in his heart that the suggestion of Ralph was true.

It was over six months before Jacob Peters was successful in getting a place, and then he had to go into a third-rate establishment, where the opportunity for advancement was small, and where his associates were not of the best character.

The years passed on; and Ralph continued as careful as in the beginning to preserve a good name. He was not content simply with doing right; but felt that it was a duty to himself, and to all who might, in any way be dependent on him, to appear right also. He was, therefore, particular in regard to the company he kept and the places he visited. Jacob, on the, contrary, continued to let inclination rather than prudence govern him in these matters. His habits were probably as good as those of Ralph, and his business capacity fully equal. But he was not regarded with the same favor, for he was often seen in company with young men known to be of loose morals, and would occasionally, visit billiard-saloons, tenpin-alleys, and other places where men of disreputable character are found. His father, who observed Jacob closely, remonstrated with him occasionally as the boy advanced towards manhood; but Jacob put on an independent air, and replied that he went on the principle of being right with himself. "You can't," he would say, "keep free from misjudgment, do what you will. Men are always more inclined to think evil of each other than good. I do nothing that I'm ashamed of."

So he continued to go where he pleased, and to associate with whom he pleased, not caring what people might say.

It is no very easy thing for as young man to make his way in the world. All the avenues to success are thickly crowded with men of talent, industry, and energy, and many favorable circumstances must conspire to help him who gets very far in advance. Talent and industry are wanted in, business, but the passport of a good character must accompany them, or they cannot be made rightly available to their possessor. it is, therefore, of the first importance to preserved a good name, for this, if united with ability and industry, with double your chances of success in life; for men will put confidence in you beyond what they can in others, who do not stand so fairly in common estimation.

In due time Ralph Gilpin and Jacob Peters entered the world as men, but not at equal advantage. They had learned the same business, and were both well acquainted with its details; but Ralph stood fairer in the eyes of business men, with whom he had come in contact, because he had been more careful about his reputation.

While Jacob was twenty-three years of age, he was getting a salary of one thousand dollars a year; but this was too small a sum to meet the demands that had come upon him. His father, to whom he was tenderly attached, had lost his health and failed in business. In consequence of this, the burden of maintaining the family fell almost entirely on Jacob. It would not have been felt as a burden if his income had been sufficient for their support. But it was not, unless their comfortable style of living was changed, and all shrunk together in a smaller house. He had sisters just advancing towards womanhood, and for their sakes, particularly, did he regret the stern necessity that required a change.

About this time, the death of a responsible clerk in the house of A. & L. left a vacancy to be filled, and as Jacob was in every way competent to take the position, which commanded a salary of eighteen hundred dollars he made application; Ralph Gilpin, who was a salesman in the house, said all that he could in Jacob's favor; but the latter had not been careful to preserve a good name, and this was against him. The place was one of trust, and the members of the firm, after considering the matter, decided adversely. Nothing as to fact was alleged or known. Not a word as to his conduct in life was said against him. But he had often been seen in company with young men who did not bear a solid reputation, and where doubt existed, it was not considered safe to employ him. So that good opportunity was lost - lost through his own fault.

Poor Jacob felt gloomy and disappointed for a time; talked of "fate," "bad luck," and all that kind of nonsense, when the cause of his ill-success was to be attributed solely to an unwise disregard of appearances.

"We shall have to remove," he said to his mother in a troubled way, after this disappointment. "If I had secured the situation at A. & L.'s all would have been well with us. But now nothing remains but to seek a humbler place to remain here will only involve us in debt; and that, above all things, we must avoid. I am sorry for Jane and Alice; but it can't be helped."

His mother tried to answer cheerfully and hopefully: but her words did not dispel a single shadow from his mind. A few days after this, a gentleman said to Jacob Peters, -

"I'll give you a hint of something that is coming in the way of good fortune. A gentleman, whose name I do not feel at liberty to mention, contemplates going into your business. He has plenty of capital, and wishes to unite himself with a young, active, and experienced man. Two or three have been thought of - you among the rest; find I believe it has been finally settled that Jacob Peters is to be the man. So let me congratulate you, my young friend, on this good fortune."

And he grasped the hand of Jacob, and shook it warmly. From the vale of despondency, the young man was at once elevated to the mountain-top of hope, and felt, for a time, bewildered in prospect of the good fortune awaited him.

Almost in that very hour the capitalist, to whom his friend referred, was in conversation with Mr. A., of the firm of A. & L.

"I have about concluded to associate with myself in business young Jacob Peters," said the former; "but before coming to a final conclusion, I thought it best to ask your opinion in the matter. You know the young man?"

"Yes," replied Mr. A., "I have known him in a business way for several years. We have considerable dealing with the house in which he is employed."

"What do you think of him?"

"He is a young man of decided business qualities."

"So it appear's to me. And you think favorably of him?"

"As to the business qualification I do," replied Mr. A., placing an emphasis on the word business.

"Then you do not think favorably of him in some other respect?"

Mr. A. was silent.

"I hope," said the, other, "that you will speak out plainly. This is a matter, to me, of the first importance. If you know of any reason why I should not associate this young man with me in business I trust you will speak without reserve."

Mr. A. remained silent for some moments, and then said, -

"I feel considerably embarrassed in regard to this matter. I would on no account give a wrong impression in regard to the young man. He may be all right; is all right, perhaps; but -"

"But what, sir?"

"I have seen him in company with young men whose

characters are not fair. And I have seen him entering into and coming out of places where it is not always safe to go."

"Enough, sir, enough!" said the gentleman, emphatically, "The matter is settled. It may be all right with him, as you say. I hope it is. But he can never be a partner of mine. And now, passing from him, I wish to ask about another young man, who has been in my mind second to Peters. He is in your employment."

"Ralph Gilpin, you mean."

"Yes."

"In every way unexceptionable. I can speak of him with the utmost confidence. He is right in all respects - right as to the business quality, right as to character, and right as to associations. You could not have a better man."

"The matter is settled, then," replied the gentleman. "I will take Ralph Gilpin if neither you nor he objects."

"There will be no objection on either side, I can answer for that," said Mr. A., and the interview closed.

From the mountain-top of hope, away down into the dark vale of despondency, passed Jacob Peters, when it was told him that Ralph Gilpin was to be a partner in the new firm which he had expected to enter.

"And so nothing is left to us," he said to himself, in bitterness of spirit, "but go down, while others, no better than we are, move steadily upwards. Why should Ralph Gilpin be preferred before me? He has no higher ability nor stricter integrity. He cannot be more faithful, more earnest, or more active than I would have been in the new position. But I am set aside and he is taken. It is a bitter, bitter disappointment!"

Three years have passed, and Ralph Gilpin is on the road to fortune, while Jacob Peters remains a clerk. And why? The one was careful of his good name; the other was not.

My young reader, take the lesson to heart. Guard well your good name; and as name signifies quality, by all means guard your spirit, so that no evil thing enter there; and your good name shall be only the expression of your good quality.

X

LITTLE LIZZIE

"IF they wouldn't let him have it!" said Mrs. Leslie, weeping. "O, if they wouldn't sell him liquor, there'd be no trouble! He's one of the best of men when he doesn't drink. He never brings liquor into the house; and he tries hard enough, I know, to keep sober, but he cannot pass Jenks's tavern."

Mrs. Leslie was talking with a sympathizing neighbor, who responded, by saying, that she wished the tavern would burn down, and that, for her part, she didn't feel any too good to apply fire to the place herself. Mrs. Leslie sighed, and wiped away the tears with her checked apron.

"It's hard, indeed, it is," she murmured, "to see a man like Jenks growing richer and richer every day out of the earnings of poor working-men, whose families are in want of bread. For every sixpence that goes over his counter some one is made poorer - to some heart is given a throb of pain."

"It's a downright shame!" exclaimed the neighbor, immediately. "If I had my way with the lazy, good-for-nothing fellow, I'd see that he did something useful, if it was to break stone on the road. Were it my husband, instead of yours, that he enticed into his bar, depend on't he'd get himself into trouble."

While this conversation was going on, a little girl, not over ten years of age, sat listening attentively. After a while she went quietly from the room, and throwing her apron over head, took her way, unobserved by her mother, down the road.

Where was little Lizzie going? There was a purpose in her mind: She had started on a mission. "O, if they wouldn't sell him liquor!" These earnest, tearful words of her, mother had filled her thoughts. If Mr. Jenks wouldn't sell her father anything to drink, "there would be no more trouble." How simple, how direct the remedy! She would go to Mr. Jenks, and ask him not to let her father have any more liquor, and then all would be well again. Artless, innocent child! And this was her mission.

The tavern kept by Jenks, the laziest man in Milanville, - he was too lazy to work, and therefore went to tavern-keeping, - stood nearly a quarter of a mile from the poor tenement occupied by the Leslies. Towards this point, under a hot, sultry sun, little Lizzie made her way, her mind so filled with its purpose that she was unconscious of heat of fatigue.

Not long before a traveller alighted at the tavern. After giving directions to have his horses fed, he entered the bar-room, and went to where Jenks stood, behind the counter.

"Have something to drink?" inquired the landlord.

"I'll take a glass of water, if you please."

Jenks could not hide the indifference at once felt towards the stranger. Very deliberately he set a pitcher and a glass upon the counter, and then turned partly away. The stranger poured out a tumbler of water, and drank it off with an air of satisfaction.

"Good water, that of yours, landlord," said he.

"Is it?" was returned, somewhat uncourteously.

"I call it good water - don't you?"

"Never drink water by itself." As Jenks said this, he winked to one of his good customers, who was lounging, in the bar. "In fact, it's so long since I drank any water, that I forgot how it tastes. Don't you, Leslie?"

The man, to whom this was addressed, was not so far lost to shame as Jenks. He blushed and looked confused, as he replied, -

"It might be better for some of us if we had not lost our relish for pure water."

"A true word spoken, my friend!" said the stranger, turning to the man, whose swollen visage, and patched, threadbare garments, too plainly told the story of his sad life. "'Water, pure water, bright water;' that is my motto. It never swells the face, nor inflames the eyes, nor mars the countenance. Its attendants are health, thrift, and happiness. It takes not away the children's bread, nor the toiling wife's garments. Water! - it is one of God's chiefest blessings! Our friend, the landlord here, says he has forgotten how it tastes; and you have lost all relish for the refreshing draught! Ah, this is a sad confession! - one which the angels might weep to hear!"

There were two or three customers in the bar besides Leslie, to whom this was addressed; and all of them, in spite of the landlord's angry and sneering countenance, treated the stranger with attention and respect. Seeing this, Jenks could not restrain himself; so, coming from behind his bar, he advanced to his side, and, laying his hand quite rudely on his shoulder, said, in a peremptory manner, -

"See here, my friend! If you are about making a temperance lecture, you can adjourn to the Town Hall or the Methodist Chapel."

The stranger moved aside a pace or two, so that the hand of Jenks might fall from his person, and then said, mildly, -

"There must be something wrong here if a man may not speak in praise of water without giving offense."

"I said you could adjourn your lecture!" The landlord's face was now fiery red, and he spoke with insolence and passion.

"O, well, as you are president of the meeting, I suppose we must let you exercise an arbitrary power of adjournment," said the stranger, good-humoredly. "I didn't think any one had so strong a dislike for water as to consider its praise an insult."

At this moment a child stepped into the bar-room. Her little face was flushed, and great beads of perspiration were slowly moving down her crimson cheeks. Her step was elastic, her manner earnest, and her large, dark eyes bright with an eager purpose. She glanced neither to the right nor the left, but walking up to the landlord, lifted to him her sweet young face, and said, in tones that thrilled every heart but his, -

"Please, Mr. Jenks, don't sell papa any more liquor!"

"Off home with you, this instant!" exclaimed Jenks, the crimson of his face deepening to a dark purple. As he spoke, he advanced towards the child, with his hand uplifted in a threatening attitude.

"Please don't, Mr. Jenks," persisted the child, not moving from where she stood, nor taking her eyes front the landlord's countenance. "Mother says, if you wouldn't sell him liquor, there'd be no trouble. He's kind and good to us all when he doesn't drink."

"Off, I say!" shouted Jenks, now maddened beyond self-control; and his hand was about descending upon the little one, when the stranger caught her in his arms, exclaiming, as he did so, with deep emotion, -

"God bless the child! No, no, precious one!" he added; "don't fear him. Plead for your father - plead for your home. Your petition must prevail! He cannot say nay to one of the little ones, whose angels do always behold the face of their Father in heaven. God bless the child!" added the stranger, in a choking voice. "O, that the father, for whom she has come on this touching errand, were present now! If there were anything of manhood yet left in his nature, this would awaken it from its palsied sleep."

"Papa! O, papa!" now cried the child, stretching forth

her hands. In the next moment she was clinging to the breast of her father, who, with his arms clasped tightly around her, stood weeping and mingling his tears with those now raining from the little one's eyes.

What an oppressive stillness pervaded that room! Jenks stood subdued and bewildered, his state of mental confusion scarcely enabling him to comprehend the full import of the scene. The stranger looked on wonderingly, yet deeply affected. Quietly, and with moist eyes, the two or three drinking customers who had been lounging in the bar, went stealthily out; and the landlord, the stranger and the father and his child, were left the only inmates of the room.

"Come, Lizzie, dear! This is no place for us," said Leslie, breaking the deep silence. "We'll go home."

And the unhappy inebriate took his child by the hand, and led her towards the door. But the little one held back.

"Wait, papa; wait!" she said. "He hasn't promised yet. O, I wish he would promise!"

"Promise her, in Heaven's name!" said the stranger.

"Promise!" said Leslie, in a stern yet solemn voice, as he turned and fixed his eyes upon the landlord.

"If I do promise, I'll keep it!" returned Jenks, in a threatening tone, as he returned the gaze of Leslie.

"Then, for God's sake, *promise!*" exclaimed Leslie, in a half-despairing voice. "*Promise, and I'm safe!*"

"Be it so! May I be cursed, if ever I sell you a drop of drinking at this bar, while I am landlord of the 'Stag and Hounds'!" Jenks spoke with with an angry emphasis.

"God be thanked!" murmured the poor drunkard, as he led his child away. "God be thanked! There is hope for me yet."

Hardly had the mother of Lizzie missed her child, ere she entered, leading her father by the hand.

"O, mother!" she exclaimed, with a joy-lit countenance, and in a voice of exultation, "Mr. Jenks has promised."

"Promised what?" Hope sprung up in her heart, on wild and fluttering wings, her face flushed, and then grew deadly pale. She sat panting for a reply.

"That he would never sell me another glass of liquor," said her husband.

A pair of thin, white hands were clasped quickly together, an ashen face was turned upwards, tearless eyes looked their thankfulness to heaven.

"There is hope yet, Ellen," said Leslie.

"Hope, hope! And O, Edward, you have said the word!"

"Hope, through our child. Innocence has prevailed over vice and cruelty. She came to the strong, evil, passionate man, and, in her weakness and innocence, prevailed over him. God made her fearless and eloquent."

A year afterwards a stranger came again that way, and stopped at the "Stag and Hounds." As before, Jenks was behind his well-filled bar, and drinking customers came and went in numbers. Jenks did not recognize him until he called for water, and drank a full tumbler of the pure liquor with a hearty zest. Then he knew him, but feigned to be ignorant of his identity. The stranger made no reference to the scene he had witnessed there a twelvemonth before, but lingered in the bar for most of the day, closely observing every one that came to drink. Leslie was not among the number.

"What has become of the man and the little girl I saw here, at my last visit to Milanville?" said the stranger, speaking at last to Jenks.

"Gone to the devil, for all I care," was the landlord's rude answer, as he turned off from his questioner.

"For all you care, no doubt," said the stranger to himself. "Men often speak their real thoughts in a passion."

"Do you see that little white cottage away off there, just at the edge of the wood? Two tall poplars stand in front."

Thus spoke to the stranger one who had heard him address the landlord.

"I do. What of it?" he answered.

"The man you asked for lives there."

"Indeed!"

"And what is more, if he keeps on as he has begun, the cottage will be all his own in another year. Jenks, here, doesn't feel any good blood for him, as you may well believe. A poor man's prosperity is regarded as so much loss to him. Leslie is a good mechanic - one of the best in Milanville. He can earn twelve dollars a week, year in and year out. Two hundred dollars he has already paid on his cottage; and as he is that much richer, Jenks thinks himself just so much poorer; for all this surplus, and more too, would have gone into his till, if Leslie had not quit drinking."

"Aha! I see! Well, did Leslie, as you call him, ever try to get a drink here, since the landlord promised never to let him have another drop?"

"Twice to my knowledge."

"And he refused him?"

"Yes. If you remember, he said, in his anger, '*May I be cursed*, if I sell him another drop.'"

"I remember it very well."

"That saved poor Leslie. Jenks is superstitious in some things. He wanted to get his custom again, - for it was well worth having, - and he was actually handing him the bottle one day, when I saw it, and reminded him of his self-imprecation. He hesitated, looked frightened, withdrew the bottle from the counter, and then, with curses, drove Leslie from his bar-room, threatening, at the same time, to horsewhip him if ever he set a foot over his threshold again."

"Poor drunkards!" mused the stranger, as he rode past the neat cottage of the reformed man a couple of hours afterwards. "As the case now stands, you are only saved as by fire. All law, all protection, is on the side of those who are engaged in enticing you into sin, and destroying you, body and soul. In their evil work, they have free course. But for you, unhappy wretches, after they have robbed you of worldly goods, and even manhood itself, are provided prisons and pauper homes! And for your children," - a dark shadow swept over the stranger's face, and a shudder went through his frame. "Can it be, a Christian country in which I live, and such things darken the very sun at noonday!" he added as he sprung his horse into a gallop and rode swiftly onward.

XI

ALICE AND THE PIGEON

ONE evening in winter as Alice, a dear little girl whom everybody loved, pushed aside the curtains of her bedroom window, she saw the moon half hidden by great banks of clouds, and only a few stars peeping out here and there. Below, the earth lay dark, and cold. The trees looked like great shadows.

There was at change in her sweet face as she let fall the curtain and turned from the window.

"Poor birds!" she said.

"They are all safe," answered her mother, smiling. "God has provided for every bird a place of rest and shelter, and each one knows where it is and how to find it. Not many stay here in the winter time, but fly away to the sunny south, where the air is warm and the trees green and fruitful."

"God is very good," said the innocent child. Then she knelt with folded hands, and prayed that her heavenly further would bless everybody, and let his angels take care of her while she slept. Her mother's kiss was still warm upon her lips as she passed into the world of pleasant dreams.

In the morning, when Alice again pushed back the curtains from her window, what a sight of wonder and beauty met her eyes! Snow had fallen, and everything wore a garment of dazzling whiteness. In the clear blue sky, away in the cast, the sun was rising; and as his beams fell upon the fields, and trees, and houses, every object glittered as if covered all over with diamonds.

But only for a moment or two did Alice look upon this beautiful picture, for a slight movement drew her eyes to a corner of the window-sill, on the outside, and there sat a pigeon close against the window-pane, with its head drawn down and almost hidden among the feathers, and its body shivering with cold. The pigeon did not seem to be afraid of her, though she saw its little pink eyes looking right into her own.

"O, poor, dear bird!" she said in soft, pitying tones, raising the window gently, so that it might not be frightened away. Then she stepped back and waited to see if the bird would not come in. Pigeon raised its brown head in a half scared away; turned it to this side and to that; and after looking first at the, comfortable chamber and then away at the snow-covered earth, quietly hopped upon the sill inside. Next he flew upon the back of a chair, and then down upon the floor.

"Little darling," said Alice, softly. Then she dressed herself quickly, and went down stairs for some crumbs of bread, which she scattered on the floor. The pigeon picked them up, with scarcely a sign of fear.

As soon as he had eaten up all the crumbs, he flew back towards the window and resting on the sill, swelled his glossy throat and cooed his thanks to his little friend. After which darted away, the morning sunshine glancing from wings.

A feeling of disappointment crept into the heart of Alice as the bird swept out of sight. "Poor little darling!" she sighed. "If he had only known how kind I would have been, and how safe he was here, what nice food and pure water would have been given, he wouldn't have flown away."

When Alice told about the visit of pigeon, at breakfast time, a pleasant surprise was felt by all at the table. And they talked of, doves and wood-pigeons, her father telling her once or two nice stories, with which she was delighted. After breakfast, her mother took a volume from the library containing Willis's exquisite poem, "The little Pigeon," and gave it to Alice to read. She soon knew it all by heart.

A great many times during the day Alice stood at the open door, or looked from the windows, in hope of seeing the pigeon again. On a distant house-top, from which the snow had been melted or blown away, or flying through the air, she would get sight of a bird now and then; but she couldn't tell whether or not it was the white and brown pigeon she had sheltered and fed in the morning. But just before sundown, as she stood by the parlor window, a cry of joy fell from her lips. There was the pigeon sitting on a fence close by, and looking, it seemed to her, quite forlorn.

Alice threw open the window, and then ran into the kitchen for some crumbs of bread. When she came back, pigeon was still on the fence. Then she called to him, holding out her her hand scattering a few crumbs on the window-sill. The bird was hungry and had sharp eyes, and when he saw Alice he no doubt remembered the nice meal she had given him in the morning, in a few moments he flew to the window, but seemed half afraid. So Alice stood a little back in the room, when he began to pick up the crumbs. Then she came nearer and nearer, holding out her hand that was full of crumbs, and as soon as pigeon had picked up all that was on the sill, he took the rest of his evening meal from the dear little girl's hand. Every now and then he would stop and look up at his kind friend, as much as to say, "Thank you for my nice supper. You are so good!" When he had eaten enough, he cooed a little, bobbed his pretty head, and then lifted his wings and flew away.

He did not come back again. At first Alice, was disappointed, but this soon wore off, and only a feeling of pleasure remained.

"I would like so much to see him and feed him," she said. "But I know he's better off and happier at his own home, with a nice place to sleep in and plenty to eat, than sitting on a window-sill all night in a snow storm." And then she would say over that sweet poem, "The City Pigeon," which her mother had given her to get by heart. Here it is, and I hope every one of my little readers will get it by heart also: -

"Stoop to my window, thou beautiful dove!
Thy daily visits have touched my love.
I watch thy coming, and list the note
That stirs so low in thy mellow throat,
And my joy is high
To catch the glance of thy gentle eye.

"Why dost thou sit on the heated eaves,
And forsake the wood with its freshened leaves?

Why dost thou haunt the sultry street,
When the paths of the forest are cool and sweet?
How canst thou bear
This noise of people - this sultry air?

"Thou alone of the feathered race
Dost look unscared on the human face;
Thou alone, with a wing to flee,
Dost love with man in his haunts to be;
And the 'gentle dove'
Has become a name for trust and love.

"A holy gift is thine, sweet bird!
Thou'rt named with childhood's earliest word!
Thou'rt linked with all that is fresh and wild
In the prisoned thoughts of the city child;
And thy glossy wings
Are its brightest image of moving things.

"It is no light chance. Thou art set apart,
Wisely by Him who has tamed thy heart,
To stir the love for the bright and fair
That else were sealed in this crowded air
I sometimes dream
Angelic rays front thy pinions stream.

"Come then, ever, when daylight leaves
The page I read, to my humble eaves,
And wash thy breast in the hollow spout,
And murmur thy low sweet music out!
I hear and see
Lessons of heaven, sweet bird, in thee!"

XII

DRESSED FOR A PARTY

A LADY sat reading. She was so absorbed in her book as to be nearly motionless. Her face, in repose, was serious, almost sad; for twice a score of years had not passed without leaving the shadow of a cloud or the mark of a tempest. The door opened, and, as she looked up, pleasant smile lay softly on her lips. A beautiful girl, elegantly attired for an evening party, came in.

"All ready?" said the lady, closing her volume, and looking at the maiden with a lively interest, that blended thoughtfulness with affection.

"All ready," aunt Helen. "And now what do you think of me? What is the effect?" Tone, expression, and manner, all gave plainly enough speaker's own answer to her questions. She thought the make up splendid - the effect striking.

"Shall I say just what I think, Alice?"

A thin veil of shadows fell over the bright young countenance.

"Love will speak tenderly. But even tenderly-spoken

things, not moving with the current of our feelings, are not pleasant to hear."

"Say on, aunt Helen. I can listen to anything from you. You think me overdressed. I see it in your eyes."

"You have read my thought correctly, dear."

"In what particular am I overdressed? Nothing could be simpler than a white illusion."

"Without an abundance of pink trimming, it would be simple and becoming enough. Your dressmaker has overloaded it with ribbon; at least, so it appears to me. But, passing that let me suggest a thought touching those two heavy bracelets. One, on the exposed arm, is sufficiently attractive. Two will create the impression that you are weakly fond of ornament; and in the eyes of every one who feels this, the effect of your dress will be marred. Men and women see down into our states of feeling with wonderful quick intuitions, and read us while we are yet ignorant in regard to ourselves."

Alice unclasped, with a faint sigh, one of the bracelets, and laid it on her aunt's bureau.

"Is that better?" she asked.

"I think so."

"But the arm is so naked, aunt. It wants something, just for relief."

"To me the effect would be improved if arms and neck were covered. But, as it is, if you think something required to draw attention from the bare skin, let one ornament be the most simple in your jewel box. You have a bracelet of hair, with neat mountings. Take that."

Alice stood for a while pondering her aunt's suggestion. Then, with half-forced cheerfulness of tone, she answered, -

"May be you're right, I'll take the hair bracelets instead. And now, what else?"

"The critic's task is never for me a pleasant one, Alice. Least pleasant when it touches one I love. If you had not asked what I thought of your appearance, I would have intruded no exceptions. I have been much in society since I was very young, and have always been an observer. Two classes of women, I notice, usually make up the staple of our social assemblages: those who consult taste in dress, and those who study effect; those who think and appreciate, and those who court admiration. By sensible people, - and we need not pay much regard to the opinion of others, - these two classes are well understood, and estimated at their real value."

"It is quite plain, aunt Helen," said Alice, her color much heightened, "that you have set me over to the side of those who study effect and court admiration."

"I think you are in danger of going over to that side, my dear," was gently answered, "and I love you too well not to desire something better for my niece. Turn your thought inward and get down, if possible, to your actual state of mind. Why have you chosen this very effective style of dress? It is not in good taste - even you, I think, will agree with me so far."

"Not in good taste, aunt Helen!"

"A prima donna, or a ballet -"

"How, aunt!" Alice made a quick interruption.

"You see, my child, how I am affected. Let me say it out in plain words - your appearance, when, you came in a few minutes ago actually shocked me."

"Indeed, indeed, aunt Helen, you are too severe in your tastes! We are not Friends."

"You are not going in the character of a May queen, Alice, that you should almost hide your beautiful hair in ribbons and flowers. A stiff bouquet in a silver holder is simply an impediment, and does not give a particle of true womanly grace. That necklace of pearls, if half hidden among soft laces, would be charming; but banding the uncovered neck and half-exposed chest, it looks bald, inharmonious, and out of place. White, with a superfluity of pink trimming, jewelry and flowers, I call on the outside of good taste; and if you go as you are, you will certainly attract all eyes, but I am sure you will not win admiration for these things from a single heart whose regard is worth having. Don't be hurt with me, Alice. I am speaking with all love and sincerity, and from a wider experience and observation than it is possible for you to have reached. Don't go as you are, if you can possibly make important changes. What time is left?"

Alice stood silent, with a clouded face. Her aunt looked at her watch.

"There is a full half hour. You may do much in that time. But you had best refer to your mother. Her taste and mine may not entirely accord."

"O, as to that, mother is on your side. But she is always so plain in her notions," said Alice, with a slight betrayal of impatience.

"A young lady will always be safest in society, Alice - always more certain to make a good impression, if she subordinate her love of dress and ornament as much as possible to her mother's taste. In breaking away from this, my dear, you have gone over to an extreme that, if persisted in, will class you with vain lovers of admiration; with mere show girls, who, conscious of no superior moral and mental attractions, seek to win by outward charms. Be not of them, dear Alice, but of the higher class, whose minds are clothed in beautiful garments whose loveliest and most precious things are, like jewels, shut within a casket."

Alice withdrew, silent, almost hurt, though not offended, and more than half resolved to give up the party. But certainly recollections checked this forming resolve before it reached a state of full decision.

"How will this do?" She pushed open the door of her aunt's room half an hour afterwards with this sentence on her lips. Her cheeks were glowing, and her eyes full of sparkles. So complete was the change, that for a brief space the aunt gazed at her wonderingly. She wore a handsome fawn-colored silk, made high in the neck, around which was a narrow lace collar of exceeding fineness, pinned with a single diamond. A linked band of gold, partly hidden by the lace undersleeve, clasped one of her wrists. A small spray of pearls and silver formed the only ornament for her hair, and nestled, beautifully contrasted among its dark and glossy braids.

"Charming!" replied aunt Helen, in no feigned admiration. "In my eyes you are a hundred times more attractive than you were, a little while ago, and will prove more attractive to all whose favor is worth the winning." And she arose and kissed her nice lovingly.

"I am not overdressed." Alice smiled.

"Better underdressed than overdressed, always, my dear, If there is any fault, it is on the right side."

"I am glad you are pleased, aunt Helen."

"Are you not better pleased with yourself?" was asked.

"I can't just say that, aunt. I've worn this dress in company several times, and it's very plain."

"It is very becoming, dear; and we always appear to best advantage in that which most accords with our style of person and complexion. To my eyes, in this more simple yet really elegant apparel, you look charming. Before, you impressed me with a sense of vulgarity; now, the impression, is one of refinement."

"Thank you for such flattering words, aunt Helen. I will accept the pictures in your eyes as justly contrasted. Of one thing I am sure, I shall feel more at ease, and less conscious of observation, than would have been the case had I gone in my gayer attire. Good evening. It is growing late, and I must be away."

The maiden stooped, and kissed her aunt affectionately.

"Good evening, dear, and may the hours be pleasant ones."

When Alice entered the drawing-room, where the company were assembling her eyes were almost dazzled with the glitter of jewelry and the splendor of colors. Most of the ladies present seemed ambitious of display, emulous of ornament. She felt out of place, in her grave and simple costume, and moved to a part of the room where she would be away from observation. But her eyes were soon wandering about, scanning forms and faces, not from simple curiosity, but with an interest that was visible in her countenance. She looked for the presence of one who had been, of late, much in her thoughts: of one for whose eyes, more than for the eyes of any other, she apparelled herself with that studied effect which received so little approval from her aunt Helen. Alice felt sober. If she entertained doubts touching her change of dress they were gone now. Plainly, to her convictions, aunt Helen was wrong and she had been wrong in yielding her own best judgement of the case.

Alice had been seated only for a little while, when she saw the young man to whom we have just referred. He was standing at the extreme end of the room, talking in a lively manner with a gayly-dressed girl, who seemed particularly pleased with his attentions. Beside her Alice would have seemed almost Quaker-like in plainness. And Alice felt this with something like a pang. Soon they passed across the room, approaching very near, and stood within a few feet of her for several minutes. Then they moved away, and sit down together not far off, still chatting in the lively manner at first observed. Once or twice the young man appeared to look directly at Alice, but no sign of recognition was visible on his face.

After the first emotions of disappointment in not being recognized had subsided, the thoughts of Alice began to lift her out of the state in much she bad been resting.

"If fine feathers make the fine bird," she said to herself, "let him have the gay plumage. As for me, I ask a higher estimate. So I will be content."

With the help of pride she rose above the weakness that was depressing her. A lady friend joined her at the moment, and she was soon interested in conversation.

"Excuse me for a personal reference, Alice," said this friend in a familiar way, "and particularly for speaking of dress. But the fact is, you shame at least one half of us girls by your perfect subordination of everything to good taste. I never saw you so faultlessly attired in my life."

"The merit, if there is any," replied Alice, "is not mine. I was coming like a butterfly, but my aunt Helen, who is making us a visit, objected so strongly that I took off my party dress and head-dress, made for the occasion, and, in a fit of half-don't-care desperation, got myself up after this modest fashion that you are pleased to call in such good taste."

"Make your aunt Helen my compliments, and say to her that I wish she were multiplied a thousands times. You will be the belle to-night, if there are many sensible man present. Ah, there comes Mr. Benton!"

At this name the heart of Alice leaped. "He has spied you out already. You are the attraction, of course, not me."

Mr. Benton, who had been, of late, so much in her thought, now stood bowing before the two young ladies, thus arresting their conversation. The last speaker was right. Alice had drawn him across the room, as was quickly apparent, for to her alone he was soon addressing himself. To quite the extent allowable in good breeding, was Alice monopolized by Mr. Benton during the evening and when he left her, with scarcely-concealed reluctance, another would take his place, and enjoy the charm of her fine intelligence.

"Have you been introduced to Alice T -?" she heard one gentleman ask of another, as she stood near a window opening into the conservatory, and partly hidden by curtains.

"Yes," was the answer.

"She is a pleasant girl."

"By odds the most charming I have met to-night. And then she has had the good taste to dress in a modest, womanly manner. How beautifully she contrasts with a dozen I could name, all radiant with colors as a bed of tulips."

She heard no more. But this was enough.

"You had a pleasant evening judging from your face," said aunt Helen, when she meet her niece on the next morning.

"Yes; it was a very pleasant one - very pleasant." Her color deepened and her eyes grew brighter.

"You were not neglected on account of you attractive style of dress?"

"Judging from the attentions I received, it must have been very attractive. A novelty, perhaps. You understand human nature better than I do, aunt Helen."

"Was it the plainest in the room?"

"It was plainer than that of half a dozen ladies old enough to have grandchildren."

The aunt smiled.

"Then it has not hurt your prospects?"

The question was in jest; but aunt Helen saw instantly into the heart of her niece. For a moment their eyes lingered in each other; then Alice looked down upon the floor.

"No it has not hurt my prospects." The answer was in a softer voice, and then followed a long-drawn inspiration, succeeded by the faintest of sighs.

A visit from Mr. Benton, on the next evening, removed all doubt from the dress question, if any remained.

XIII

COFFEE vs. BRANDY

"WE shall have to give them a wedding party," said Mrs. Eldridge to her husband.

Mr. Eldridge assented.

"They will be home to-morrow, and I think of sending out of invitations for Thursday."

"As you like about that," replied Mr. Eldridge. "The trouble will be yours."

"You have no objections?"

"O, none in the world. Fanny is a good little girl, and the least we can do is to pay her this compliment on her marriage. I am not altogether satisfied about her husband, however; he was rather a wild sort of a boy a year or two ago."

"I guess he's all right now," remarked Mrs. Eldridge; "and he strikes me as a very kind-hearted, well-meaning young man. I have flattered myself that Fanny has done quite well as the average run of girls."

"Perhaps so," said Mr. Eldridge, a little thoughtfully.

"Will you be in the neighborhood of Snyder's?" inquired the lady.

"I think not. We are very busy just now, and I shall hardly have time to leave the store to-day. But I can step around there to-morrow."

"To-morrow, or even the next day, will answer," replied Mrs. Eldridge. "You must order the liquors. I will attend to everything else."

"How many are you going to invite?" inquired Mr. Eldridge.

"I have not made out a list yet, but it will not fall much short of seventy or eighty."

"Seventy or eighty!" repeated Mr. Eldridge.

"Let me see. Three dozen of champagne; a dozen of sherry; a dozen of port; a dozen of hock, and a gallon of brandy, - that will be enough to put life into them I imagine."

"Or death!" Mrs. Eldridge spoke to herself, in an undertone.

Her husband, if he noticed the remark, did not reply to it, but said, "Good morning," and left the house. A lad about sixteen years of age sat in the room during this conversation, with a book in his hand and his eyes on the page before him. He did not once look up or move; and an observer would have supposed him so much interested in his book as not to have heard the passing conversation. But he had listened to every word. As soon as Mr. Eldridge left the room his book fell upon his lap, and looking towards Mrs. Eldridge, he said, in an earnest but respectful manner, -

"Don't have any liquor, mother."

Mrs s Eldridge looked neither offended nor irritated by this remonstrance, as she replied, -

"I wish it were possible to avoid having liquor, my son; but it is the custom of society and if we give a party it must be in the way it is done by other people."

This did not satisfy the boy, who had been for some time associated with the Cadets of Temperance, and he answered, but with modesty and great respect of, manner, - "If other people do wrong, mother - what then?"

"I am not so sure of its being wrong, Henry."

"O, but mother," spoke out the boy, quickly, "if it hurts people to drink, it must be wrong to give them liquor. Now I've been thinking how much better it would be to have a nice cup of coffee. I am sure that four out of five would like it a great deal better than wine or brandy. And nobody could possibly receive any harm. Didn't you hear what father said about Mr. Lewis? That he had been rather wild? I am sure I shall never forget seeing him stagger in the street once. I suppose he has reformed. But just think, if the taste should be revived again and at our house, and he should become intoxicated at this wedding party! O, mother! It makes me feel dreadfully to think about it. And dear Cousin Fanny! What sorrow it would bring to her!"

"O, dear, Henry! Don't talk in that kind of a way! You

make me shudder all over. You're getting too much carried away by this subject of temperance"

And Mrs. Eldridge left the room to look after her domestic duties. But she could not push from her mind certain uneasy thoughts which her son's suggestions had awakened. During the morning an intimate lady friend came in to whom Mrs. Eldridge spoke of the intended party.

"And would you believe it," she said, "that old-fashioned boy of mine actually proposed that we should have coffee instead of wine and brandy."

"And you're going to adopt the suggestion," replied the lady, her face lighten up with a pleasant smile.

"It would suit my own views exactly; but then such an innovation upon a common usage as that; is not to be thought of for a moment."

"And why not?" asked the lady. "Coffee is safe, while wine and brandy are always dangerous in promiscuous companies. You can never tell in what morbid appetite you may excite an unhealthy craving. You may receive into your house a young man with intellect clear, and moral purposes well-balanced, and send him home at midnight, to his mother, stupid from intoxication! Take your son's advice, my friend. Exclude the wine and brandy, and give a pleasant cup of coffee to your guests instead."

"O, dear, no, I can't do that!" said Mrs. Eldridge. "It would look as if we were too mean to furnish wines and brandy. Besides, my husband would never consent to it."

"Let me give you a little experience of my own. It may help you to a right decision in this case."

The lady spoke with some earnestness, and a sober cast of thought in her countenance. "It is now about three years since I gave a large party, at which a number of young men were present, - boys I should rather say. Among these was the son of an old and very dear friend. He was in his nineteenth year, - a handsome, intelligent, and most agreeable person - full of life and pleasant humor. At supper time I noticed him with a glass of champagne in his hand, gayly talking with some ladies. In a little while after, my eyes happening to rest on him, I saw him holding, a glass of port wine to his lips, which was emptied at a single draught. Again passing near him, in order to speak to a lady, I observed a tumbler in his hand, and knew the contents to be brandy and water. This caused me to feel some concern, and I kept him, in closer observation. In a little while he was at the table again, pouring out another glass of wine. I thought it might be for a lady upon whom he was in attendance; but no, the sparkling liquor touched his own lips. When the company returned to the parlors, the flushed face, swimming eyes, and over-hilarious manner of my young friend, showed too plainly that he had been drinking to excess. He was so much excited as to attract the attention of every one, and his condition became the subject of remark. He was mortified and distressed at the occurrence, and drawing him from the room, made free to tell him the truth. He showed some indignation at first, and intimated that I had insulted him but I rebuked him sternly, and told him he had better go home. I was too much excited to act very wisely. He took me at my word, and left the house. There was no sleep for my eyes on that night, Mrs. Eldridge. The image of that boy going home to his mother at midnight, in such a condition, and made so by my hand haunted me like a rebuking spectre; and I resolved never again to set out a table with liquors to a promiscuous company of young and old, and I have kept that word of promise. My husband is not willing to have a party unless there is wine with the refreshments, and I would rather forego all entertainments than put temptation in the way of any one. Your son's suggestion is admirable. Have the independence to act upon it, and set an example which many will be glad to follow. Don't fear criticism or remark; don't stop to ask what this one will say or that one think. The approval of our own consciences is worth far more than the opinions of men. Is it right? That is the question to ask; not How will it appear? or What will people say? There will be a number of parties given to your niece, without doubt; and if you, lead off with coffee instead of wine, all the rest of Fanny's friends may follow the good example."

When Mr. Eldridge came home at dinner-time, his wife said to him, -

"You needn't order any liquors from Snyder."

"Why not?" Mr. Eldridge looked at his wife with some surprise.

"I'm going to have coffee, instead of wine, and brandy," said Mrs. Eldridge, speaking firmly.

"Nonsense!" You're jesting."

"No, I'm in earnest. These liquors are not only expensive, but dangerous things to offer freely in mixed companies. Many boys get their first taste for drink at fashionable parties, and many reformed men have the old fiery thirst revived by a glass of wine poured out for them in social hospitality. I am afraid to have my conscience burdened with the responsibility which this involves."

"There is no question as to the injury that is done by this free pouring out of liquors at our fashionable entertainments. I've long enough seen that," said Mr. Eldridge; "but she will be a bold lady who ventures to offer a cup of coffee in place of a glass of wine. You had better think twice on this subject before you act once."

"I've done little else I but think about it for the last two hours, and the more I think about it the more settled my purpose becomes."

"But what put this thing into your head?" inquired Mr. Eldridge. "You were in full sail for party this morning, liquor and all; this sudden tacking for a new course is a little surprising. I'm puzzled."

"Your son put it into my head," replied Mrs. Eldridge.

"Henry? Well, that boy does beat all!" Mr. Eldridge did not speak with disapprobation, but with a tone of pleasure in his voice. "And so he proposed that we should have coffee instead of wine and brandy?"

"Yes."

"Bravo for Henry! I like that. But what will people say, my dear? I don't want to become a laughing stock."

"I'd rather have other people laugh at me for doing right," said Mrs. Eldridge, "than to have my conscience blame me for doing wrong."

"Must we give the party?" asked Mr. Eldridge, who did not feel much inclined to brave public opinion.

"I don't see that we can well avoid doing so. Parties will be given, and as Fanny is our niece, it will look like a slight towards her if we hold back. No, she must have a party; and as I am resolved to exclude liquor, we must come in first. Who knows but all the rest may follow our example."

"Don't flatter yourself on any such result. We shall stand alone, you may depend upon it."

The evening of the party came and a large company assembled at the house of Mr. and Mrs. Eldridge. At eleven o'clock they passed to the supper-room. On this time the thoughts of the host and hostess had passed, ever and anon, during the whole evening, and not without many misgivings as to the effect their entertainment would produce on the minds of the company. Mr. Eldridge was particularly nervous on the subject. There were several gentlemen present whom he knew to be lovers of good wine; gentlemen at whose houses he had often been entertained, and never without the exhilarating glass. How would they feel? What would they think? What would they say? These questions fairly haunted him; and he regretted, over and over again, that he had yielded to his wife and excluded the liquors.

But there was no holding back now; the die was cast, and they must stand to the issue. Mr. Eldridge tried to speak pleasantly to the lady on his arm, as he ascended to the supper-room; but the words came heavily from his tongue, for his heart was dying in him. Soon the company were around the table, and eyes, critical in such matters, taking hurried inventories of what it contained. Setting aside the wine and brandy, the entertainment was of the most liberal character, and the whole arrangement extremely elegant. At each end of the table stood a large coffee-urn, surrounded with cups, the meaning of which was not long a mystery to the company. After the terrapin, oysters, salad, and their accompaniments, Mr. Eldridge said to a lady, in a half-hesitating voice, as if he were almost ashamed to ask the question, -

"Will you have a cup of coffee?"

"If you please," was the smiling answer. "Nothing would suit me better."

"Delicious!" Mr. Eldridge heard one of the gentlemen, of whom he stood most in dread, say. "This is indeed a treat. I wouldn't give such a cup of coffee for the best glass of wine you could bring me."

"I am glad you are pleased," Mr. Eldridge could not help remarking, as he turned to the gentleman.

"You couldn't have pleased me better," was replied.

Soon the cups were circling through the room, and every one seemed to enjoy the rich beverage. It was not the ghost of coffee, nor coffee robbed of its delicate aroma; but clear, strong, fragrant, and mellowed by the most delicious cream. Having elected to serve coffee, Mrs. Eldridge was careful that her entertainment should not prove a failure through any lack of excellence in this article. And it was very far from proving a failure. The first surprise being over, one and another began to express an opinion on the subject to the host and hostess.

"Let me thank you," said a lady, taking the hand of Mrs. Eldridge, and speaking very warmly, "for your courage in making this innovation upon a custom of doubtful prudence. I thank you, as a mother, who has two sons here to-night."

She said no more, but Mrs. Eldridge understood well her whole meaning.

"You are a brave man, and I honor you," was the remark of a gentleman to Mr. Eldridge. "There will be many, I think, to follow your good example. I should never have had the courage to lead, but I think I shall be brave enough to follow, when it comes my turn to entertain my friends."

Henry was standing by his father when this was said listening with respectful, but deeply gratified attention.

"My son, sir," said Mr. Eldridge.

The gentleman took the boy by the hand, and while he held it, the father added, -

"I must let the honor go to where it really is due. The suggestion came from him. He is a Cadet of Temperance, and when the party was talked of, he pleaded so earnestly for the substitution of coffee for wine and brandy, and used such good reason for the change, that we saw only one right course before us, and that we have adopted."

The gentleman, on hearing this, shook the lad's hand warmly, and said, -

"Your father has reason to be proud of you, my brave boy! There is no telling what good may grew out of this thing. Others will follow your father's example, and hundreds of young men be saved from the enticements of the wine cup."

With what strong throbs of pleasure did the boy's heart beat when these words came to his ears! He had scarcely hoped for success when he pleaded briefly, but earnestly, with his mother. Yet he felt that he must speak, for to his mind, what she proposed doing was a great evil. Since it had been resolved to banish liquor from the entertainment, he had heard his father and mother speak several times doubtfully as to the result; and more than once his father expressed result that any such "foolish" attempt to run in the face of people's prejudices had been thought of. Naturally, he had felt anxious about the result; but now that the affair had gone off so triumphantly, his heart was outgushing with pleasure.

The result was as had been predicted. Four parties were given to the bride, and in each case the good example of Mrs. Eldridge was followed. Coffee took the place of wine and brandy, and it was the remark of nearly all, that there had been no pleasant parties during the season.

So much for what a boy may do, by only a few right words spoken at the right time, and in the right manner. Henry Eldridge was thoughtful, modest, and earnest-minded. His attachment to the cause of temperance was not a mere boyish enthusiasm, but the result of a conviction that intemperance was a vice destructive, to both soul and body, and one that lay like a curse and a plague-spot on society, He could understand how, if the boys rejected, entirely, the cup of confusion, the next, generation of men would be sober; and this had led him to join the Cadets, and do all in his power to get other lads to join also. In drawing other lads into the order, he had been very successful; and now, in a few respectfully uttered, but earnest words, he had checked the progress of intemperance in a circle far beyond the ordinary reach of his influence.

Henry Eldridge was a happy boy that night.

XIV

AMY'S QUESTION

"AMY!"

Mrs. Grove called from the door that opened towards the garden. But no answer came. The sun had set half an hour before, and his parting, rays, were faintly tinging with gold and purple few clouds that lay just alone the edge of the western sky. In the east, the full moon was rising in all her beauty, making pale the stars that were sparking in the firmament.

"Where is Amy?" she asked. "Has any one seen her come in?"

"I saw her go up stairs with her knitting in her hand half an hour ago," said Amy's brother, who was busily at work with his knife on a block of pine wood, trying to make a boat.

Mrs. Grove went to the foot of the stairs, and called again. But there was no reply.

"I wonder where the child can be," she said to herself, a slight feeling of anxiety crossing her mind. So she went up stairs to looks for her. The door of Amy's bedroom was shut, but on pushing it open Mrs. Grove saw her little girl sitting at the open window, so lost in the beauty of the moonlit sky and her own thoughts that she did not hear the noise of her mother's entrance.

"Amy," said Mrs. Grove.

The child started, and then said quickly, -

"O, mother! Come and see! Isn't it lovely?"

"What are you looking at, dear?" asked Mrs. Grove, as she sat down by her side, and drew an arm around her.

"At the moon, and stars, and the lake away off by the hill. See what a great road of light lies across the water! Isn't it beautiful, mother? And it makes me feel so quiet and happy. I wonder why it is?"

"Shall I tell you the reason?"

"O, yes, mother, dear! What is the reason?"

"God made everything that is good and beautiful."

"O, yes, I know that!"

"Good and beautiful for the sake of man; because man is the highest thing of creation and nearest to God. All things below him were created for his good; that is, God made them for him to use in sustaining the life of his body or the life of his soul."

"I don't see what use I can make of the moon and stars," said Amy.

"And yet," answered her mother, "you said only a

minute ago that the beauty of this moon-light evening made you feel so quiet and happy."

"O, yes! That is so; and you were going to tell me why it was."

"First," said the mother, "let me, remind you that the moon and stars give us light by night, and that, if you happened to be away at a neighbor's after the sun went down, they would be of great use in showing you the path home-ward."

"I didn't think of that when I spoke of not seeing what use I could make, of the moon and stars," Amy replied.

Her mother went on, -

"God made everything that is good and beautiful for the stake of man, as I have just told you; and each of these good and beautiful things of creation comes to us with a double blessing, - one for our bodies and the other for our souls. The moon and stars not only give light this evening to make dark ways plain, but their calm presence fills our souls with peace. And they do so, because all things of nature being the work of God, have in them a likeness of something in himself not seen by our eyes, but felt in our souls. Do you understand anything of what I mean, Amy?"

"Just a little, only," answered the child. "Do you mean, mother dear, that God is inside of the moon and stars, and everything else that he has made?"

"Not exactly what I mean; but that he has so made them, that each created thin is as a mirror in which our souls may see something of his love and his wisdom reflected. In the water we see an image of his truth, that, if learned, will satisfy our thirsty minds and cleanse us from impurity. In the sun we see an image of his love, that gives light, and warmth, and all beauty and health to our souls."

"And what in the moon?" asked Amy.

"The moon is cold and calm, not warm and brilliant like the sun, which tells us of God's love. Like truths learned, but not made warm and bright by love, it shows us the way in times of darkness. But you are too young to understand much about this. Only keep in your memory that every good and beautiful thing you see, being made by God, reflects something of his nature and quality to your soul and that this is why the lovely, the grand, the beautiful, the pure, and sweet things of nature fill your heart with peace or delight when you gaze at them."

For a little while after this they sat looking out of the window, both feeling very peaceful in the presence of God and his works. Then voice was heard below, and Amy, starting up, exclaimed, -

"O, there is father!" and taking her mother's hand, went down to meet him.

XV

AN ANGEL IN DISGUISE

IDLENESS, vice, and intemperance had done their miserable work, and the dead mother lay cold and still amid her wretched children. She had fallen upon the threshold of her own door in a drunken fit, and died in the presence of her frightened little ones.

Death touches the spring of our common humanity. This woman had been despised, scoffed at, and angrily denounced by nearly every man, woman, and child in the village; but now, as the fact of, her death was passed from lip to lip, in subdued tones, pity took the place of anger, and sorrow of denunciation. Neighbors went hastily to the old tumble-down hut, in which she had secured little more than a place of shelter from summer heats and winter cold: some with grave-clothes for a decent interment of the body; and some with food for the half-starving children, three in number. Of these, John, the oldest, a boy of twelve, was a stout lad, able to earn his living with any farmer. Kate, between ten and eleven, was bright, active girl, out of whom something clever might be made, if in good hands; but poor little Maggie, the youngest, was hopelessly diseased. Two years before a fall from a window had injured her spine, and she had not been able to leave her bed since, except when lifted in the arms of her mother.

"What is to be done with the children?" That was the chief question now. The dead mother would go underground, and be forever beyond all care or concern of the villagers. But the children must not be left to starve. After considering the matter, and talking it over with his wife, farmer Jones said that he would take John, and do well by him, now that his mother was out of the way; and Mrs. Ellis, who had been looking out for a bound girl, concluded that it would be charitable in her to make choice of Katy, even though she was too young to be of much use for several years.

"I could do much better, I know," said Mrs. Ellis; "but as no one seems inclined to take her, I must act from a sense of duty expect to have trouble with the child; for she's an undisciplined thing - used to having her own way."

But no one said "I'll take Maggie." Pitying glances were cast on her wan and wasted form and thoughts were troubled on her account. Mothers brought cast-off garments and, removing her soiled and ragged clothes, dressed her in clean attire. The sad eyes and patient face of the little one touched many hearts, and even knocked at them for entrance. But none opened to take her in. Who wanted a bed-ridden child?

"Take her to the poorhouse," said a rough man, of whom the question "What's to be done with Maggie?" was asked. "Nobody's going to be bothered with her."

"The poorhouse is a sad place for a sick and helpless child," answered one.

"For your child or mine," said the other, lightly speaking; "but for tis brat it will prove a blessed change, she will be kept clean, have healthy food, and be doctored, which is more than can be said of her past condition."

There was reason in that, but still it didn't satisfy. The day following the day of death was made the day of burial. A few neighbors were at the miserable hovel, but none followed dead cart as it bore the unhonored remains to its pauper grave. Farmer Jones, after the coffin was taken out, placed John in his wagon and drove away, satisfied that he had done his part. Mrs. Ellis spoke to Kate with a hurried air, "Bid your sister good by," and drew the tearful children apart ere scarcely their lips had touched in a sobbing farewell. Hastily others went out, some glancing at Maggie, and some resolutely refraining from a look, until all had gone. She was alone! Just beyond the threshold Joe Thompson, the wheelwright, paused, and said to the blacksmith's wife, who was hastening off with the rest, -

"It's a cruel thing to leave her so."

"Then take her to the poorhouse: she'll have to go there," answered the blacksmith's wife, springing away, and leaving Joe behind.

For a little while the man stood with a puzzled air; then he turned back, and went into the hovel again. Maggie with painful effort, had raised herself to an upright position and was sitting on the bed, straining her eyes upon the door out of which all had just departed, A vague terror had come into her thin white face.

"O, Mr. Thompson!" she cried out, catching her suspended breath, "don't leave me here all alone!"

Though rough in exterior, Joe Thompson, the wheelwright, had a heart, and it was very tender in some places. He liked children, and was pleased to have them come to his shop, where sleds and wagons were made or mended for the village lads without a draft on their hoarded sixpences.

"No, dear," he answered, in a kind voice, going to the bed, and stooping down over the child, "You sha'n't be left here alone." Then he wrapped her with the gentleness almost of a woman, in the clean bedclothes which some neighbor had brought; and, lifting her in his strong arms, bore her out into the air and across the field that lay between the hovel and his home.

Now, Joe Thompson's wife, who happened to be childless, was not a woman of saintly temper, nor much given to self-denial for others' good, and Joe had well-grounded doubts touching the manner of greeting he should receive on his arrival. Mrs. Thompson saw him approaching from the window, and with ruffling feathers met him a few paces from the door, as he opened the garden gate, and came in. He bore a precious burden, and he felt it to be so. As his arms held the sick child to his breast, a sphere of tenderness went out from her, and penetrated his feelings. A bond had already corded itself around them both, and love was springing into life.

"What have you there?" sharply questioned Mrs. Thompson.

Joe, felt the child start and shrink against him. He did

not reply, except by a look that was pleading and cautionary, that said, "Wait a moment for explanations, and be gentle;" and, passing in, carried Maggie to the small chamber on the first floor, and laid her on a bed. Then, stepping back, he shut the door, and stood face to face with his vinegar-tempered wife in the passage-way outside.

"You haven't brought home that sick brat!" Anger and astonishment were in the tones of Mrs. Joe Thompson; her face was in a flame.

"I think women's hearts are sometimes very hard," said Joe. Usually Joe Thompson got out of his wife's way, or kept rigidly silent and non-combative when she fired up on any subject; it was with some surprise, therefore, that she now encountered a firmly-set countenance and a resolute pair of eyes.

"Women's hearts are not half so hard as men's!"

Joe saw, by a quick intuition, that his resolute bearing had impressed his wife and he answered quickly, and with real indignation, "Be that as it may, every woman at the funeral turned her eyes steadily from the sick child's face, and when the cart went off with her dead mother, hurried away, and left her alone in that old hut, with the sun not an hour in the sky."

"Where were John and Kate?" asked Mrs. Thompson.

"Farmer Jones tossed John into his wagon, and drove off. Katie went home with Mrs. Ellis; but nobody wanted the poor sick one. 'Send her to the poorhouse,' was the cry."

"Why didn't you let her go, then. What did you bring her here for?"

"She can't walk to the poorhouse," said Joe; "somebody's arms must carry her, and mine are strong enough for that task."

"Then why didn't you keep on? Why did you stop here?" demanded the wife.

"Because I'm not apt to go on fools' errands. The Guardians must first be seen, and a permit obtained."

There was no gainsaying this.

"When will you see the Guardians?" was asked, with irrepressible impatience.

"To-morrow."

"Why put it off till to-morrow? Go at once for the permit, and get the whole thing off of your hands to-night."

"Jane," said the wheelwright, with an impressiveness of tone that greatly subdued his wife, "I read in the Bible sometimes, and find much said about little children. How the Savior rebuked the disciples who would not receive them; how he took them up in his arms, and blessed them; and how he said that 'whosoever gave them even a cup of cold water should not go unrewarded.' Now, it is a small thing for us to keep this poor motherless little one for a single night; to be kind to her for a single night; to make her life comfortable for a single night."

The voice of the strong, rough man shook, and he turned his head away, so that the moisture in his eyes might not be seen. Mrs. Thompson did not answer, but a soft feeling crept into her heart.

"Look at her kindly, Jane; speak to her kindly," said Joe. "Think of her dead mother, and the loneliness, the pain, the sorrow that must be on all her coming life." The softness of his heart gave unwonted eloquence to his lips.

Mrs. Thompson did not reply, but presently turned towards the little chamber where her husband had deposited Maggie; and, pushing open the door, went quietly in. Joe did not follow; he saw that, her state had changed, and felt that it would be best to leave her alone with the child. So he went to his shop, which stood near the house, and worked until dusky evening released him from labor. A light shining through the little chamber windows was the first object that attracted Joe's attention on turning towards the house: it was a good omen. The path led him by this windows and, when opposite, he could not help pausing to look in. It was now dark enough outside to screen him from observation. Maggie lay, a little raised on the pillow with the lamp shining full upon her face. Mrs. Thompson was sitting by the bed, talking to the child; but her back was towards the window, so that her countenance was not seen. From Maggie's face, therefore, Joe must read the character of their intercourse. He saw that her eyes were intently fixed upon his wife; that now and then a few words came, as if in answers from her lips; that her expression was sad and tender; but he saw nothing of bitterness or pain. A deep-drawn breath was followed by one of relief, as a weight lifted itself from his heart.

On entering, Joe did not go immediately to the little chamber. His heavy tread about the kitchen brought his wife somewhat hurriedly from the room where she had been with Maggie. Joe thought it best not to refer to the child, nor to manifest any concern in regard to her.

"How soon will supper be ready?" he asked.

"Right soon," answered Mrs. Thompson, beginning to bustle about. There was no asperity in her voice.

After washing from his hands and face the dust and soil of work, Joe left the kitchen, and went to the little bedroom. A pair of large bright eyes looked up at him from the snowy bed; looked at him tenderly, gratefully, pleadingly. How his heart swelled in his bosom! With what a quicker motion came the heart-beats! Joe sat down, and now, for the first time, examining the thin free carefully under the lamp light, saw that it was an attractive face, and full of a childish sweetness which suffering had not been able to obliterate.

"Your name is Maggie?" he said, as he sat down and took her soft little hand in his.

"Yes, sir." Her voice struck a chord that quivered in a low strain of music.

"Have you been sick long?"

"Yes, sir." What a sweet patience was in her tone!

"Has the doctor been to see you?"

"He used to come."

"But not lately?"

"No, sir."

"Have you any pain?"

"Sometimes, but not now."

"When had you pain?"

"This morning my side ached, and my back hurt when you carried me."

"It hurts you to be lifted or moved about?"

"Yes, sir."

"Your side doesn't ache now?"

"No, sir."

"Does it ache a great deal?"

"Yes, sir; but it hasn't ached any since I've been on this soft bed."

"The soft bed feels good."

"O, yes, sir - so good!" What a satisfaction, mingled with gratitude, was in her voice!

"Supper is ready," said Mrs. Thompson, looking into the room a little while afterwards.

Joe glanced from his wife's face to that of Maggie; she understood him, and answered, -

"She can wait until we are done; then I will bring her somethings to eat." There was an effort at indifference on the part of Mrs. Thompson, but her husband had seen her through the window, and understood that the coldness was assumed. Joe waited, after sitting down to the table, for his wife to introduce the subject uppermost in both of their thoughts; but she kept silent on that theme, for many minutes, and he maintained a like reserve. At last she said, abruptly, -

"What are you going to do with that child?"

"I thought you understood me that she was to go to the poorhouse," replied Joe, as if surprised at her question.

Mrs. Thompson looked rather strangely at her husband for sonic moments, and then dropped her eyes. The subject was not again referred to during the meal. At its close, Mrs. Thompson toasted a slice of bread, and softened, it with milk and butter; adding to this a cup of tea, she took them into Maggie, and held the small waiter, on which she had placed them, while the hungry child ate with every sign of pleasure.

"Is it good?" asked Mrs. Thompson, seeing with what a keen relish the food was taken.

The child paused with the cup in her hand, and answered with a look of gratitude that awoke to new life old human feelings which had been slumbering in her heart for half a score of years.

"We'll keep her a day or two longer; she is so weak and helpless," said Mrs. Joe Thompson, in answer to her husband's remark, at breakfast-time on the next morning, that he must step down and see the Guardians of the Poor about Maggie.

"She'll be so much in your way," said Joe.

"I sha'n't mind that for a day or two. Poor thing!"

Joe did not see the Guardians of the Poor on that day, on the next, nor on the day following. In fact, he never saw them at all on Maggie's account, for in less than a week Mrs. Joe Thompson would as soon leave thought of taking up her own abode in the almshouse as sending Maggie there.

What light and blessing did that sick and helpless child bring to the home of Joe Thompson, the poor wheelwright! It had been dark, and cold, and miserable there for a long time just because his wife had nothing to love and care for out of herself, and so became soar, irritable, ill-tempered, and self-afflicting in the desolation of her woman's nature. Now the sweetness of that sick child, looking ever to her in love, patience, and gratitude, was as honey to her soul, and she carried her in her heart as well as in her arms, a precious burden. As for Joe Thompson, there was not a man in all the neighborhood who drank daily of a more precious wine of life than he. An angel had come into his house, disguised as a sick, helpless, and miserable child, and filled all its dreary chambers with the sunshine of love.

XVI

WHICH WAS MOST THE LADY?

"DID you ever see such a queer looking figure?" exclaimed a young lady, speaking loud enough to be heard by the object of her remark. She was riding slowly along in an open carriage, a short distance from the city, accompanied by a relative. The young man, her companion, looked across the, road at a woman, whose attire was certainly not in any way very near approach to the fashion of the day. She had on a faded calico dress, short in the waist; stout leather shoes; the remains of what had once been a red merino long shawl, and a dingy old Leghorn bonnet of the style of eighteen hundred and twenty.

As the young man turned to look at the woman, the latter raised her eyes and fixed them steadily upon the young lady who had so rudely directed towards her the attention of her companion. Her face, was not old nor faded, as the dress she wore. It was youthful, but plain almost to homeliness; and the smallness of her eyes, which were close together and placed at the Mongolian angle, gave to her countenance a singular aspect.

"How do you do, aunty?" said the young man gently drawing on the rein of his horse so as still further to diminish his speed.

The face of the young girl - for she was quite young - reddened, and she slackened her steps so as to fall behind the rude, unfeeling couple, who sought to make themselves merry at her expense.

"She is gypsy!" said the young lady, laughing.

"Gran'mother! How are catnip and hoarhound, snakeroot and tansy, selling to-day? What's the state of the herb market?" joined the young man with increasing rudeness.

"That bonnet's from the ark - ha! ha!"

"And was worn by the wife of Shem, Ham or Japheth. Ha! now I've got it! This is the great, great, great granddaughter of Noah. What a discovery! Where's Barnum? Here's a chance for another fortune!"

The poor girl made no answer to this cruel and cowardly assault, but turned her face away, and stood still, in order to let the carriage pass on.

"You look like a gentleman and a lady," said a man whom was riding by, and happened to overhear some of their last remarks; "and no doubt regard yourselves as such. But your conduct is anything but gentlemanly and lady-like; and if I had the pleasure of knowing your friends, I would advise them to keep you in until you had sense and decency enough not to disgrace yourselves and them!"

A fiery spot burned instantly on the young man's face, and fierce anger shot from his eyes. But the one who had spoken so sharply fixed upon him a look of withering contempt, and riding close up to the carriage, handed him his card, remarking coldly, as he did so, -

"I shall be pleased to meet you again, sir. May I ask your card in return?"

The young man thrust his hand indignantly into his pocket, and fumbled there for some moments, but without finding a card.

"No matter," said he, trying to speak fiercely; "you will hear from me in good time."

"And you from me on the spot, if I should happen to catch you at such mean and cowardly work as you were just now engaged in," said the stranger, no seeking to veil his contempt.

"The vulgar brute! O, he's horrid!" ejaculated the young lady as her rather crestfallen companion laid the whip upon his horse and dashed ahead. "How he frightened me!"

"Some greasy butcher or two-fisted blacksmith," said the elegant young man with contempt. "But," he added boastfully, "I'll teach him a lesson!"

Out into the beautiful country, with feeling a little less buoyant than when they started, rode our gay young couple. As the excitement of passion died away both feel a little uncomfortable in mind, for certain unpleasant convictions intruded themselves, and certain precepts in the code of polite usage grew rather distinct in their memories. They had been thoughtless, to say the least of it.

"But the girl looked so queer!" said the young lady. "I

couldn't help laughing to save my life. Where on earth did she come from?"

Not very keen was their enjoyment of the afternoon's ride, although the day was particularly fine, and their way was amid some bits of charming scenery. After going out into the country some five or six miles, the horse's head was turned, and they took their way homeward. Wishing to avoid the Monotony of a drive along the same road the young man struck across the country in order to reach another avenue leading into the city, but missed his way and bewildered in a maze of winding country roads. While descending a steep hill, in a very secluded place, a wheel came off, and both were thrown from the carriage. The young man received only a slight bruise, but the girl was more seriously injured. Her head had struck against a stone with so strong a concussion as to render her insensible.

Eagerly glancing around for aid, the young man saw, at no great distance from the road, a poor looking log tenement, from the mud chimney of which curled a thin column of smoke, giving signs of inhabitants. To call aloud was his first impulse, and he raised his voice with the cry of "Help!"

Scarcely had the sound died away, ere he saw the door of the cabin flung open, and a woman and boy looked eagerly around.

"Help!" he cried again, and the sound of his voice directed their eyes towards him. Even in his distress, alarm, and bewilderment, the young man recognized instantly in the woman the person they had so wantonly insulted only an hour or two before. As soon as she saw them, she ran forward hastily, and seeing the white face of the insensible girl, exclaimed, with pity and concern, -

"O, sir! is she badly hurt?"

There was heart in that voice of peculiar sweetness.

"Poor lady!" she said, tenderly, as she untied the bonnet strings with gentle care, and placed her hand upon the clammy temples.

"Shall I help you to take her over to the house?" she added, drawing an arm beneath the form of the insensible girl.

"Thank you!" There was a tone of respect in the young man's voice. "But I can carry her myself;" and he raised the insensible form in his arms, and, following the young stranger, bore it into her humble dwelling. As he laid her upon a bed, he asked, eagerly, -

"Is there a doctor near?"

"Yes, sir," replied the girl. "If you will come to the door, I will show you the doctor's house; and I think he must be at home, for I saw him go by only a quarter of an hour since. John will take care of your horse while you are away, and I will do my best for the poor lady."

The doctor's house, about a quarter of a mile distant, was pointed out, and the young man hurried off at a rapid speed. He was gone only a few minutes when his insensible companion revived, and, starting up, looked wildly around her.

"Where am I? Where is George?" she asked, eagerly.

"He has gone for the doctor; but will be back very soon," said the young woman, in a kind, soothing voice.

"For the doctor! Who's injured?" She had clasped her hands across her forehead, and now, on removing them, saw on one a wet stain of blood. With a frightened cry she fell backs upon the pillow from which she had risen.

"I don't think you are much hurt," was said, in a tone of encouragement, as with a damp cloth the gentle stranger wiped very tenderly her forehead. "The cut is not deep. Have you pain anywhere?"

"No," was faintly answered.

"You can move your arms; so *they* are uninjured. And now, won't you just step on to the floor, and see if you can bear your weight? Let me raise you up, There, put your foot down - now the other - now take a step - now another. There are no bones broken! How glad I am!"

How earnest, how gentle, how pleased she was. There was no acting in her manner. Every tone, expression, and gesture showed that heart was in everything.

"O, I am glad!" she repeated. "It might have been so much worse."

The first glance into the young girl's face was one of identification; and even amid the terror that oppressed her heart, the unwilling visitor felt a sense of painful mortification. There was no mistaking that peculiar countenance. But how different she seemed! Her voice was singularly sweet, her manner gentle and full of kindness, and in her movements and attitude a certain ease that marked her as one not to be classed, even by the over-refined young lady who was so suddenly brought within her power, among the common herd.

All that assiduous care and kind attention could do for the unhappy girl, until the doctor's arrival, was done. After getting back to the bed from which she bad been induced to rise, in order to see if all her limbs were sound, she grew sick and faint, and remained so until the physician came. He gave it as his opinion that she had received some internal injuries, and that it would not be safe to attempt her removal.

The young couple looked at each other with dismay pictured in their countenances.

"I wish it were in my power to make you more comfortable," said the kind-hearted girl, in whose humble abode they were. "What we have is at your service in welcome, and all that it is in my power to do shall be done for you cheerfully. If father was only at home - but that can't be helped."

The young man dazed upon her in wonder and shame - wonder at the charm that now appeared in her singularly marked countenance, and shame for the disgraceful and cowardly cruelty with which he had a little while before so wantonly assailed her.

The doctor was positive about the matter, and so there was no alternative. After seeing his unhappy relative in as comfortable a condition as possible, the young man, with the doctor's aid, repaired his crippled vehicle by the restoration of a linchpin, and started for the city to bear intelligence of the sad accident, and bring out the mother of the injured girl.

Alone with the person towards whom she had only a short time before acted in such shameless violation of womanly kindness and lady-like propriety, our "nice young lady" did not feel more comfortable in mind than body. Every look - every word - every tone - every act of the kind-hearted girl - was a rebuke. The delicacy of her attentions, and the absence of everything like a desire to refund her of the recent unpleasant incident, marked her as possessing, even if her face and attire were plain, and her position humble, all the elements of a true lady.

Although the doctor, when he left, did not speak very encouragingly, the vigorous system of the young girl began to react and she grew better quite rapidly so that when her parents arrived with the family physician, she was so much improved that it was at once decided to take her to the city.

For an hour before her parents came she lay feigning to be in sleep, yet observing every movement and word of her gentle attendant. It was an hour of shame, self-reproaches, and repentance. She was not really bad at heart; but false estimates of things, trifling associations, and a thoughtless disregard of others, had made her far less a lady in act than she imagined herself to be in quality. Her parents, when they arrived, overwhelmed the young girl with thankfulness; and the father, at parting, tried to induce her to accept a sum of money. But the offers seemed to disturb her.

"O, no, sir!" she said, drawing back, while a glow came into her pale face, and made it almost beautiful; "I have only done a simple duty."

"But you are poor," he urged, glancing around. "Take this, and let it make you more comfortable."

"We are contented with what God has given to us," she replied, cheerfully. "For what he gives is always the best portion. No, sir; I cannot receive money for doing only a common duty."

"Your reward is great," said the father, touched with the noble answer, "may God bless you, my good girl! And if you will not receive my money, accept my grateful thanks."

As the daughter parted from the strange young girl, she bent down and kissed her hand; then looking up into her face, with tearful eyes, she whispered for her ears alone, -

"I am punished, and you are vindicated. O, let your heart forgive me!"

"It was God whom you offended," was whispered back. "Get his forgiveness, and all will be right. You have mine, and also the prayer of my heart that you may be good and wise, for only such are happy."

The humbled girl grasped her hand tightly, and murmured, "I shall never forget you - never!"

Nor did she. If the direct offer of her father was declined, indirect benefits reached, through her means, the lonely log cottage, where everything in time put on a new and pleasant aspect, wind the surroundings of the gentle spirit that presides there were more in agreement with her true internal quality. To the thoughtless young couple the incidents of that day were a life-lesson that never passed entirely from their remembrance. They obtained a glance below the surface of things that surprised them, learning that, even in the humblest, there may be hearts in the right places - warm with pure feelings, and inspired by the noblest sentiments of humanity; and that highly as they esteem themselves on account of their position, there was one, at least, standing below them so far as external advantages were concerned, who was their superior in all the higher qualities that go to make up the real lady and gentleman.

XVII

OTHER PEOPLE'S EYES

"OUR parlor carpet is beginning to look real shabby," said Mrs. Cartwright. "I declare! if I don't feel right down ashamed of it, every time a visitor, who is anybody, calls in to see me."

"A new one will cost -"

The husband of Mrs. Cartwright, a good-natured, compliant man, who was never better pleased than when he could please his wife, paused to let her finish the sentence, which she did promptly, by saying, -

"Only forty dollars. I've counted it all up. It will take thirty-six yards. I saw a beautiful piece at Martin's - just the thing - at one dollar a yard. Binding, and other little matters, won't go beyond three or four dollars, and I can make it myself, you know."

"Only forty dollars! Mr. Cartwright glanced down at the carpet which had decorated the floor of their little parlor for nearly five years. It had a pleasant look in his eyes, for it was associated with many pleasant memories. Only forty dollars for a new one! If the cost were only five, instead of forty, the inclination to banish this old friend to an out-of-the-way chamber would have been no stronger in the mind of Mr. Cartwright. But forty dollars was an item in the calculation, and to Mr. Cartwright a serious one. Every year he was finding it harder to meet the gradually increasing demand upon his purse; for there was a steadily progressive enlargement of his family, and year after year the cost of living advanced. He was thinking of this when his wife said, -

"You know, Henry, that cousin Sally Gray is coming here on a visit week after next. Now I do want to put the very best face on to things while she is here. We were married at the same time, and I hear that her husband is getting rich. I feel a little pride about the matter, and don't want her to think that we're growing worse off than when we began life, and can't afford to replace this shabby old carpet by a new one." No further argument was needed. Mr. Cartwright had sixty dollars in one of the bureau drawers, - a fact well known to his wife. And it was also well known to her that it was the accumulation of very careful savings, designed, when the sum reached one hundred dollars, to cancel a loan made by a friend, at a time when sickness and a death in the family had run up their yearly expenses beyond the year's income. Very desirous was Mr. Cartwright to pay off this loan, and he had felt lighter in heart as those aggregate of his savings came nearer and nearer to the sum required for that purpose.

But he had no firmness to oppose his wife in anything. Her wishes in this instance, as in many others, he unwisely made a law. The argument about cousin Sally Gray was irresistible. No more than his wife did he wish to look poor in her eyes; and so, for the sake of her eyes, a new carpet was bought, and the old one -

not by any means as worn and faded as the language of his wife indicated - sent up stairs to do second-hand duty in the spare bedroom.

Not within the limit of forty dollars was the expense confined. A more costly pattern than could be obtained for one dollar a yard tempted the eyes of Mrs. Cartwright, and abstracted from her husband's savings the sum of over fifty dollars. Mats and rugs to go with the carpet were indispensable, to give the parlor the right effect in the eyes of cousin Sally Gray, and the purchase of these absorbed the remainder of Mr. Cartwright's carefully hoarded sixty dollars.

Unfortunately, for the comfortable condition of Mrs. Cartwright's mind, the new carpet, with its flaunting colors, put wholly out of countenance the cane-seat chairs and modest pier table, and gave to the dull paper on the wall a duller aspect. Before, she had scarcely noticed the hangings on the Venetian blinds, now, it seemed as if they had lost their freshness in a day; and the places where they were broken, and had been sewed again, were singularly apparent every time her eye rested upon them.

"These blinds do look dreadfully!" she said to her husband, on the day after the carpet went down. "Can you remember what they cost?"

"Eight dollars," replied Mr. Cartwright.

"So much?" The wife sighed as she spoke.

"Yes, that was the price. I remember it very well."

"I wonder what new hangings would cost?" Mrs.

Cartwright's manner grew suddenly more cheerful, as the suggestion of a cheaper way to improve the windows came into her thought.

"Not much, I presume," answered her husband.

"Don't you think we'd better have it done?"

"Yes," was the compliant answer.

"Will you stop at the blind-maker's, as you go to the store, and tell him to send up for them to-day? It must be attended to at once, you know, for cousin Sally will be here on next Wednesday."

Mr. Cartwright called at the blind-maker's, as requested, and the blind-maker promised to send for the blinds. From there he continued onto the store in which he was employed. There he found a note on his desk from the friend to whom he was indebted for the one hundred dollars.

"Dear Cartwright" (so the note ran), "if it is possible for you to let me have the one hundred dollars I loaned you, its return to-morrow will be a particular favor, as I have a large payment to make, and have been disapp-ointed in the receipt of a sum of money confidently expected."

A very sudden change of feeling did Mr. Cartwright experience. He had, in a degree, partaken of his wife's pleasure in observing the improved appearances of their little parlor but this pleasure was now succeeded by a sense of painful regret and mortification. It was nearly two hours before Mr. Cartwright returned an answer to his friend's note. Most of that time had been spent in the vain effort to discover some way out of the difficulty in which he found himself placed. He would have asked an advance of one hundred dollars on his salary, but he did not deem that a prudent step, and for two reasons. One was, the known character of his employers; and the other was involved in the question of how he was to support his family for the time he was working out this advance? At last, in sadness and humiliation, he wrote a brief reply, regretting his inability to replace the loan now, but promising to do it in a very short time. Not very long after this answer was sent, there came another note from his friend, written in evident haste, and under the influence of angry feelings. It was in these words: -

"I enclose your due bill, which I, yesterday, thought good for its face. But, as it is worthless, I send it back. The man who buys new carpets and new furniture, instead of paying his honest debts, can be no friend of mine. I am sorry to have been mistaken in Henry Cartwright."

Twice did the unhappy man read this cutting letter; then, folding it up slowly, be concealed it in one of his pockets. Nothing was said about it to his wife, whose wordy admiration of the new carpet, and morning, noon, and night, for the next two or three days, was a continual reproof of his weakness for having yielded to her wishes in a matter where calm judgement and a principle of right should have prevailed. But she could not help noticing that he was less cheerful; and once or twice he spoke to her in a way that she thought positively ill-natured. Something was wrong with him; but what that something was, she did not for an instant imagine.

At last the day arrived for cousin Sally Gray's visit. Unfortunately the Venetian blinds were still at the blind-maker's, where they were likely to remain for a week longer, as it was discovered, on the previous afternoon, that he had never touched them since they came into his shop. Without them the little parlor had a terribly bare look; the strong light coming in, and contrasting harshly the new, gaudy carpet with the old, worn, and faded furniture. Mrs. Cartwright fairly cried with vexation.

"We must have something for the windows, Henry," she said, as she stood, disconsolate, in the parlor, after tea. "It will never do in the world to let cousin Sally find us in this trim."

"Cousin Sally will find a welcome in our hearts," replied her husband, in a sober voice, "and that, I am sure, will be more grateful to her than new carpets and window blinds."

The way in which this was spoken rather surprised Mrs. Cartwright, and she felt just a little rebuked.

"Don't you think," she said, after a few moments of silence on both sides, "that we might afford to buy a few yards of lace to put up to the windows, just for decency's sake?"

"No," answered the husband, firmly. "We have afforded too much already."

His manner seemed to Mrs. Cartwright almost ill-natured. It hurt her very much. Both sat down in the parlor, and both remained silent. Mrs. Cartwright thought of the mean appearance everything in that "best room" would have in the eyes of cousin Sally, and Mr. Cartwright thought of his debt to his friend, and of that friend's anger and alienation. Both felt more uncomfortable than they had been for a long time.

On the next day cousin Sally arrived. She had not come to spy out the nakedness of the land, - not for the purpose of making contrasts between her own condition in life and that of Mr. Cartwright, - but from pure love. She had always been warmly attached to her cousin; and the years during which new life-associations had separated them had increased rather than diminished this attachment. But the gladness of their meeting was soon overshadowed; at least for cousin Sally. She saw by the end of the first day's visit that her cousin was more concerned to make a good appearance in her eyes, - to have her understand that she and her husband were getting along bravely in the world, - than to open her heart to her as of old, and exchange with her a few pages in the history of their inner lives. What interest had she in the new carpet, or the curtainless window, that seemed to be the most prominent of all things in the mind of her relative? None whatever! If the visit had been from Mary Cartwright to herself, she would never have thought for an instant of making preparations for her coming in the purchase of new furniture, or by any change in the externals of her home. All arrangements for the reception would have been in her heart.

Cousin Sally was disappointed. She did not find the relative, with whom so many years of her life had been spent in sweet intercourse, as she had hoped to find her. The girlish warmth of feelings had given place to a cold worldliness that repelled instead of attracting her. She had loved, and suffered much; had passed through many trials, and entered through many opening doors into new experiences, during the years since their ways parted. And she had come to this old, dear friend, yearning for that heart intercourse, - that reading together of some of the pages of their books of life, - which she felt almost as a necessity. What interest had she for the mere externals of Mary's life? None! None! And the constant reference thereto, by her cousin, seemed like a desecration. Careful and troubled about the little things of life, she found the dear old friend of her girlish days, to whom she had come hopefully, as to one who could comprehend, as in earlier years, the feelings, thoughts, and aspirations which had grown stronger, deeper, and of wider range.

Alas! Alas! How was the fine gold dimmed in her eyes!

"Dear Mary!" she said to her cousin, on the morning of the day that was, to end her visit, - they were sitting, together in the little parlor, and Mrs. Cartwright had referred, for the fortieth time, to the unshaded windows, and declared herself mortified to death at the appearance of things, - "Dear Mary! It was to see you, not your furniture, that I came. To look into your heart and feel it beating against mine as of old; not to pry, curiously, into your ways of living, nor to compare your house-furnishing with my own. But for your constant reference to these things, I should not have noticed, particularly, how your house was attired; and if asked about them, could only have answered, 'She's living very nicely.' Forgive me for this plain speech, dear cousin. I did not mean to give utterance to such language; but the words are spoken now, and cannot be recalled."

Mrs. Cartwright, if not really offended, was mortified and rebuked and these states of feeling united with pride, served to give coldness to her exterior. She tried to be cordial in manner towards her cousin; to seem as if she had not felt her words; but this was impossible, for she had felt them too deeply. She saw that the cherished friend and companion of her girlhood was disappointed in her; that she had come to look into her heart, and not into the attiring of her home; and was going away with diminished affection. After years of divergence, their paths had touched; and, separating once more, she felt that they would never run parallel again.

A few hours later, cousin Sally gave her a parting kiss. How different in warmth to the kiss of meeting! Very sad, very dissatisfied with herself, - very unhappy did Mrs. Cartwright feel, as she sat musing alone after her relative had departed. She was conscious of having lost a friend forever, because she had not risen to the higher level to which that friend had attained - not in external, but in the true internal life.

But a sharper mortification was in store for her. The letter of her husband's friend, in which he had returned the due bill for one hundred dollars, fell accidentally into her hands, and overwhelmed her with consternation. For that new carpet, which had failed to win more than a few extorted sentences of praise from cousin Sally Gray, her husband had lost the esteem of one of his oldest and best friends, and was now suffering, in silence, the most painful trial of his life.

Poor, weak woman! Instead of the pleasure she had hoped to gain in the possession of this carpet, it had made her completely wretched. While sitting almost stupefied with the pressure that was on her feelings, a neighbor called in, and she went down to the parlor to meet her.

"What a lovely carpet!" said the neighbor, in real admiration. "Where did you buy it?"

"At Martin's," was answered.

"Had they any more of the same pattern?" inquired the neighbor.

"This was the last piece."

The neighbor was sorry. It was the most beautiful pattern she had ever seen; and she would hunt the city over but what she would find another just like it.

"You may have this one," said Mrs Cartwright, on the impulse of the moment. "My husband doesn't particularly fancy it. Your parlor is exactly the size of mine. It is all made and bound nicely as you can see; and this work on it shall cost you nothing. We paid a little over fifty dollars for the carpet before a stitch was taken in it; and fifty dollars will make you the possessor."

"Are you really in earnest?" said the neighbor.

"Never more so in my life."

"It is a bargain, then."

"Very well."

"When can I have it?"

"Just as soon as I can rip it from the floor," said Mrs. Cartwright, in real earnest.

"Go to work," replied the neighbor, laughing out at the novelty of the affair. "Before your task is half done, I will be back with the fifty dollars, and a man to carry home the carpet."

And so she was. In less than half an hour after the sale was made, in this off-hand fashion, Mrs. Cartwright sat alone in her parlor, looking down upon the naked floor. But she had five ten-dollar gold pieces in her hand, and they were of more value in her eyes than twenty carpets. Not long did she sit musing here. There was other work to do. The old carpet must be replaced upon the parlor floor ere her husband's return. And it was replaced. In the midst of her hurried operations the old blinds with the new hangings came in, and were put up to the windows. When Mr. Cartwright returned home, and stepped inside of the little parlor, where he found his wife awaiting him, he gave an exclamation of surprise.

"Why, Mary! What is the meaning of this? Where is the new carpet?"

She laid the five gold pieces in his hand, and then looked earnestly, and with tears in her eyes, upon his wondering face.

"What are these, Mary? Where did they come from?"

"Cousin Sally is gone. The carpet didn't seem attractive in her eyes, and it has lost all beauty in mine. So I sold the unlovely thing, and here is the money. Take it, dear Henry, and let it serve the purpose for which it was designed."

"All right again!" exclaimed Mr. Cartwright, as soon as the whole matter was clear to him. "All right, Mary, dear! That carpet, had it remained, would have wrecked, I fear, the happiness of our home. Ah, let us consult only our own eyes hereafter, Mary - not the eyes of other people! None think the better of us for what we seem - only for what we are. It is not from fine furniture that our true pleasure in life is to come, but from a consciousness of right-doing. Let the inner life be right, and the outer life will surely be in just harmony. In the humble abode of virtue there is more real happiness than in the palace-homes of the unjust, the selfish, and wrong-doers. The sentiment is old as the world, but it must come to every heart, at some time in life, with all the force of an original utterance. And let it so come to us now, dear wife!"

And thus it did come. This little experience showed them an aspect of things that quickened their better reasons, and its smart remained long enough to give it the power of a monitor in all their after lives. They never erred again in this wise. For two or three years more the old carpet did duty in their neat little parlor, and when it was at last replaced by a new one, the change was made for their own eyes, and not for the eyes of another.

www.ingramcontent.com/pod-product-compliance
Lightning Source LLC
Chambersburg PA
CBHW020548310726
48979CB00008B/1140/J

* 9 7 8 1 4 2 1 8 0 0 9 3 6 *